The Reluctant Rescue

By Pitz and Mary

(aided by Stewart Ferris,
but only with the words)

Published by Accent Press Ltd 2018

ISBN 9781786151827

Printed in Great Britain by Clays Ltd, St Ives plc

Accent Press Ltd
Octavo House
West Bute Street
Cardiff
CF10 5LJ

For Mary and Pitz

Pooch

Hello. My name is Pooch and I'm the most important dog in the world and anyone who says otherwise has obviously met me.

Actually, Pooch isn't even my real name. It's Pitz, which apparently means 'small'. I find that slightly unnecessary given that I'm only thirty centimetres high. I don't need to be reminded of my stature every time someone says my name.

I'm a Yorkie, or Yorkshire Terrier to use my posh breed name. And I am posh – full pedigree, so watch it. This is my story, and you're going to love it because I'm so special and adorable and, and, well, I could go on... so I will – and handsome, and furry, and loveable and brilliant. You probably get the idea. If you don't, go back to the start of this paragraph and read it again until you do.

My name is Pooch and I'm the most important dog in the world.

Satisfied of my dazzling wondrousness? Right, I'll continue. When I was a fluffy puppy, just a few weeks old, I chose to adopt a human called Katia. The warm palm of her hand was almost a perfect fit for my tiny body, and she looked like she needed a pup like me to look after her. I took her to live with me in a house on the banks of the Hudson River, close to New York City. I trained Katia to do tricks and to obey my every command. Depending on the tone of my bark, she would know if I wanted to go outside for a pee-pee, if I was hungry, if I needed a cuddle, or if there was a wicked cat in the vicinity. I'm not sure if Katia was a pedigree, but she was quite smart for a human and I was pleased at how quickly she learned to do my bidding.

Life was good with Katia. I let her drive me around in her Lexus, and I would slobber all over the heated leather seats and make stains with my wet nose on the window. Sometimes I would let her take me to work with her so I could play on the desk and distract her colleagues. She worked in Times Square, which I recommend anyone to visit because it has some interesting sniffs and there's a particularly nice lamp post on the corner of 49th Street and Broadway if you're ever caught short.

And on that subject, my house by the Hudson had the best outdoor bathroom a dog could wish for.

There was a vast oak tree that seemed taller than the clouds. There was a lawn that stretched to the horizon. There were bushes that were alive with buzzing things. There were flower pots positioned all around the terrace and the steps that led to the river. It was always possible to find a fresh scent to enjoy whilst relieving myself.

In the spring, I made it my job to chase away the baby ducks that used to waddle in a line behind their mother. In the summer the now-enormous baby ducks got their revenge by chasing me away from the river. Autumn was a joyous cascade of leaves in which I would lose myself, and the snowy winter was my excuse for doing nothing but curl up in front of a log fire.

Though life was undeniably fun in my paradise by the Hudson, don't think I was spoiled or lazy. I played my part and made a valuable contribution to the running of the household. Occasionally there would be pigeons that needed scaring, for example, or passers-by who needed to be frightened off. I never hesitated when circumstances required me to step up and do my bit. Despite these duties, I somehow found time to play with my expensive furry toys, and I always found the energy to wake my human up at sunrise, no matter how late she had gone to bed.

If I wanted to visit the top floor of the house, I would usually get half way up the stairs and then decide I didn't really want to go all the way up after all. Normally, aborting my mission would require me to turn around and walk back down again, but such efforts were not for me. I found it more efficient to train my human to rescue me from such a predicament. All I had to do was to sit on a step and yap annoyingly. Hey presto, I was whisked into Katia's arms and deposited on a sofa. Life was perfect.

Well, not quite. There was one problem in my house. A big problem. And her name was Gabriela.

Gabriela was already living in the house when I moved in, and, for reasons I've never understood, failed to move out after my arrival. She was one of those cat things. Tabby on top with snow white fur from the neck to the paws, honey whiskers, deep, dark, thoughtful eyes, and a tail that swished with the elegance of a movie star; a picture of purity and innocence. You know the sort – they pretend to be cute, but their paws contain razor-sharp knives that will slice you into rashers of bacon. Mmm, bacon... Where was I? Yes, the problem of cats. Cats consume food. They take up space on the couch. They compete for attention from your human. In short, cats are an abomination, and Gabriela was the worst of all of them.

Let me give you an example of the dastardly things she would do to make my life miserable. Once, I was trying to get to the front door to bark madly at a random noise that I thought I'd heard. Gabriela was lying asleep across the hallway, almost entirely blocking my path. I was forced to make a slight detour, and by the time I got to the door I'd forgotten what I was doing there! I think you get the picture. What had I done to deserve a life of cohabitation with this Mephistopheles?

I decided that the cat situation was intolerable and I needed to act. The beginnings of a plan began to formulate in my mind.

There was one problem in my house. A big problem.
And her name was Gabriela.

Mary

Yo! Mary here. What a beautiful day! And how gorgeous of you to be reading this. I think I'm in love with you already, dear reader. Hmm, you do smell nice. Mind you, that might not be much of a compliment considering the sort of things I enjoy sniffing: dogs' bottoms and, well, other dogs' bottoms... but I'm delighted to be able to tell you my story. And it starts in a hot country, far away. Well, it's far if you don't live there already. Anyway, I was born in Greece. A country with abundant sunshine, thousands of islands, and rather too many stray dogs.

I was one such stray. I don't remember my parents, though I guess one of them looked a bit like a Labrador, since that's what I sort of am, albeit blended with other breeds. Dogs tend not to live very long where I come from. The winters are tough. When the beachside restaurants close, there are no scraps. I hope it wasn't too painful for my mum and dad when their food finally ran out.

My only dependable companion was hunger. *Peina*, they call it where I come from. The first part of the word sounds similar to the word 'pain', which is totally appropriate. There was never enough nourishment for all the strays in my town. As if this wasn't challenging enough, it was hard for me to hunt, because I have a minor disability: I only have one eye. It means I bump into things on my blind side and there's no point in me going to see a 3D film. Other than that, I get by just fine. Pain and hunger are all in the mind. A positive disposition enabled me to enjoy life, despite my situation. Don't you go worrying about me!

And don't you worry about the large scars on my neck. Sure, I've been treated badly. Some people are not nice to dogs, but I think that's because they don't understand that dogs have the same emotions as humans. Any human who doesn't appreciate that simple fact is probably less intelligent than a dog anyway, so if I get beaten or whipped or kicked by someone, then I don't hold it against them. It's far better to forgive.

My earliest memory is of playing on the beach, using a stick for a toy. If there wasn't a stick, I would play with sun-baked poo. I made a rather decent home for myself under a wheelie bin. It gave me shelter from the hot sun, and it kept some of the rain off me during thunderstorms. The wheelie bin was in the port town of Orei, at the edge of the Aegean Sea.

The fishing harbour would fill with sailing yachts in the summer. The boats were like giant, white fish, shiny and tasty-looking. Actually, I was often so ravenous that everything became tasty-looking. I developed a penchant for grass. Yummy stuff. Can't get enough of it. Especially when it's green and juicy, right after it's been raining. To be honest, the grass often made me sick, but at least it suppressed those hunger pangs for an hour or two.

Things would improve when a new yacht arrived. The passengers would see me sleeping on the quayside, and they would put a bowl of water out and pieces of bread and cheese. If I was really lucky I might get a slice of ham. These yacht people were wonderful to me. I would smile at them, and they would make sure that when they left Orei, ready to sail to another island, I would have a full stomach that I hoped would see me through until the next kind-hearted people arrived. I used to dream that one of those people would invite me onto their yacht and let me sail away to a new life. Dreams were important. They were the only things I had.

Pooch

Who was that interrupting me? Revolting one-eyed stray. Yuck. We're supposed to be talking about me. I'm the important one. Where was I? I get easily distracted because my brain is only the size of a walnut. I can't recall what I was saying... Mmm, walnuts. Yum. Ooh, look, a teddy bear. I think I'll play with my stuffed toy for a few minutes. It's from Macy's. Katia bought it for me. She said it cost the same as feeding a hungry animal for a month. I've never understood that comment; if you feed a hungry animal once, it's not hungry any more. So, well ... I don't know where I'm going with this, but it's my posh toy, and I'm going to throw it around the room and growl a bit. Yes, that seems like a plan. Go away and come back when I've finished.

You still there? I said go away. I'm busy. I'll deal with you when I've stopped doing whatever it was I said I was going to do.

Oh, flip. Now I've forgotten what I wanted to do while you were away. Probably something a bit naughty, knowing me. At least that smelly stray seems to have gone quiet. Can't stand dirty hounds. I have a bath regularly. Usually once a year, whether I need it or not.

Ah, just remembered. I was talking about the hideous monster that I had to share my home with. Not Katia, my human – I like her – I mean the furry thing with sharp claws; the cat monster. Gabriela. Evil thing. Used to goose-step around the kitchen giving orders and plotting to annexe the dining room.

I did what I could to make it clear Gabriela was not wanted in this house. I drank her water. I ate her food. I clearly marked all of my territory with legally-binding pee-pee. It is the duty of any dog to persecute any cat, and I did not ignore my responsibilities, but after a year of this intolerable situation, I decided to try a different tactic. One thing you learn when you're a Yorkie is that if something is plainly not working, such as scratching a door to try to get it to open, it's best to give up after about a thousand attempts. We're quick learners, we little doggies. We know when we're beaten, provided we've been failing at something for several seasons. So, I thought to myself, I have one ally in the house (Katia) and one arch enemy, who I won't name for legal reasons (Gabriela). If I can add a second ally, perhaps that will be enough to defeat the powers of darkness that threaten my domain? It seemed, appropriately for my mentality, simple.

I decided to adopt a second human.

Part of my property portfolio.

There were plenty to choose from. Normally I frightened them away with my fierce, high-pitched yapping, but I started to consider the possibility of allowing them to remain. First I thought about the garbage men. There were about four of them, and they came to the house every week to take away bags of stuff. And, yes, I had thought of persuading

Gabriela into one of those bags, but she would never fall for it. Anyway, the idea of all four garbage men moving in with me and Katia was appealing. They could form a team to protect me from the cat. They would have endless energy to throw balls for me. They could also fetch the balls for me, because I was too important for all that silly running around nonsense. Katia's bed was large enough for her to be able to share it with most of the bin men, and if any of them didn't fit in it, they could sleep on the sofa or in the spare room.

I also considered the mailman. He came to the house every day, and every day I would scare him off. It usually took him a full twenty-four hours to recover from the fright I gave him before he would dare to come again. He wouldn't fit in Katia's bed if it was already full of garbage men, but he probably wouldn't mind curling up on the rug by the fire. It was nice down there.

All I needed to do, I decided, was to cease being territorially defensive with these people, and they would stay. If I welcomed them, they would move in and be my friend. My plan was perfect. It could not fail.

But then it snowed, and everything changed.

I don't know where she found him. Maybe he was a snowman. Maybe he was lost in the snow and she picked him up in the comfy car that I let her drive me around in. Whatever it was, he walked into my home on a cold December morning and I knew I'd found my second human. How did I know? Because we had everything in common (except for intelligence and social sophistication – he was way beneath me on those scores). He picked up my favourite toy rope and threw it for me. I barked excitedly and waited for him to fetch it. He fetched it. And then he did it again. This was my favourite game, making humans throw and fetch things for me, and it turned out that this was his favourite, too. We were instantly best friends. I didn't leave his side all day. The bond we shared was based on common interests and a mutual sense of joy in playing dumb doggy games. Perhaps his brain was also the size of a walnut? But even if it wasn't as big as mine, we were meant to be together from the start. His name was Stewart and he stayed for Christmas. He was the best present a dog could wish for. Apart from a chew. Or a bone. Or a sausage. Or anything remotely edible, for that matter. Or anything squeaky.

And the good news kept coming. Stewart was allergic to cats. Couldn't stand the monsters. He forged an instant dislike to Gabriela.

I had found my ally. My life of deprivation and neglect was about to get better. Next morning, I slipped out the door and ran away down the street for no reason whatsoever. Stewart noticed I was missing and chased after me, quickly catching me up on the pavement beside the busy road. As cars and trucks thundered past, barely inches away and completely unaware of my presence, he swept me up into his arms and carried me home to safety. From then on I was convinced he was the right human to join my family and I decided to adopt him forever.

Just days later he vanished. Packed a bag and went. I wondered if it was something I had said. Was I not waking him early enough in the mornings? I always tried to get him up at dawn. Sometimes earlier. Any sooner and it would have been the night before. Did I not pee on the floor enough for him? He seemed to relish the experience of mopping up my mess. He loved it so much he would clean my pee-pee within seconds of it leaking onto the doormat or the rug. I tried my best to give him the opportunity to clean up after me as often as possible, but there's only so much a small dog can produce, and I had to save some of it for registering my real estate every day.

Brando

Oh no, the sun is out. It's looking at me in a funny way. I don't like it. What's that noise? Sounds like a child. Help me! Children frighten me. I don't like the way they move unpredictably and bounce balls around. In fact, I think kids are the most terrifying things on the planet. Apart from everything else. I think the whole world is out to get me. Life is a big conspiracy against helpless Beagles like me. I think I'd better hide in my doggy bed until all the scary sounds and lights and shadows have gone away. My name's Brando, and, what's that? Oh, I've just been told that I'm not part of this story yet. Apparently, I don't have any part to play until much later. Phew, that's a relief. I was finding all this communication a bit stressful. I'll hide under a blankie until I'm needed. Bye.

My name's Brando and I think the whole world is out to get me.

Pooch

What on earth was that? Another interruption? I will not tolerate this! There is so much I need to tell you about me, and there really isn't time for these stray mutts to butt in with their irrelevant rants. And now I've totally forgotten where I am and what my name is... Hang on, it will come back to me. Let me just go and pee on a doormat. I'll be right back.

That's better. Hope someone will clean that up soon. Don't want the house to stink. Right, what was I saying? I was probably talking about me, wasn't I? Seems fairly likely. So, me. Yes. I'm an important little hound, and I managed to acquire two humans to be my pets, but then my new human, Stewart, disappeared after a just a week. It was a new year, and things were back as they were before he arrived, just me and Katia against the forces of evil, otherwise known as Gabriela.

With Stewart gone, I thought about the garbage men and the mailman again. Perhaps I had made a mistake by not getting them to move in with Katia, but I could fix that. It wouldn't be hard to get them on my side. I tried not barking at them when they visited, but somehow I couldn't bring myself to stay silent. The fearsome yaps leapt involuntarily from my jaws. Something inside me no longer wanted any other humans. I missed Stewart, and there was nothing I could do to bring him back.

Meanwhile, the cat-induced terrorism continued. She would sleep on my favourite bit of the couch. She would play with my toys. She even drank from my water bowl. The cruelty I suffered was beyond words. My only reprieve was to go to work with Katia. Gabriela was never invited to the office. She never got to ride in the car. I enjoyed rubbing my adorable scent on the soft front seat as we made the forty-minute commute to Times Square, before spending the day distracting film editors and sound technicians and movie stars from doing whatever they were supposed to be doing. I would sit on people's desks, tread on their keyboards and walk across their control panels, ruining their work. They loved it. And I wasn't even supposed to be there. The doorman was meant to turn away any dogs, but because I'm so petite and insignificant I could sneak into the building by hiding in Katia's handbag.

Spending the day distracting film editors and sound technicians and movie stars from doing whatever they were supposed to be doing.

But, inevitably, those blissful, cat-free hours in the office would end, and Katia would chauffeur me home to the waiting claws of the jealous cat. Gabriela would be simmering with hate, having spent the entire day plotting her evil schemes. I needed help. I needed Stewart to come back.

Finally he returned, jet-lagged and carrying a suitcase. Life was good once more. It was like we were a proper family, with me at the head. I really enjoyed having two pet humans. And when Katia was at work, Stewart played with me. He made sure the cat remained where she belonged: as far away as possible. At last, everything was perfect.

And then he disappeared again! Just packed up his suitcase one morning and left. I felt guilty at letting him escape, and wondered how he would cope without me. Perhaps I should have put a lead on him? Humans need to be restrained and, with hindsight, I realised the mistake I had made in letting him run free. His absence made me feel depressed for a full twenty minutes until I forgot all about him. And despite my limited memory capacity, the joy I felt when he returned a week later was overwhelming. I was so excited I had to pee on the doormat. This routine of him visiting for a few days with his suitcase, and then going away for a week or two, became the norm. I thought further about trying to find another human or two to replace him, and was quite tempted by a team of sweaty tree surgeons who came to trim the oak in my garden, but I decided that I could cope with Stewart on a part-time basis. At least it gave me occasional reprieve from co-existing with my miserable feline foe.

The visits from Stewart continued like this for about eighteen months, which is about ten years in the proper canine timescale, then things started to change. Boxes appeared. A 'For Sale' sign hung from a post in front of the house. Katia held garage sales. She started selling her furniture and belongings. I hoped she might get an offer to buy the cat, but

Gabriela was understandably not a tempting prospect at any price. The 'For Sale' sign was replaced with 'Sold'. Finally, Katia and Stewart trapped Gabriela in a laundry bag, loaded the screaming and hissing beast into the car along with some boxes, then put me in my travel bag.

So, with absolutely no warning, we drove away from my beautiful home, never to return. Well, no warning other than numerous visits from estate agents and potential house buyers, and weeks of packing and preparation, and the day before when a whole load of muscly removal men took everything away. So, you can understand that it all came as a bit of a shock when we moved out of my riverside home and tried to squeeze everything into a small apartment in Jane Street, New York.

We were two floors up in this apartment, which is a lot for my little legs, but fortunately there was an elevator to carry me. Her name was Katia. Whenever she took me out to pee in Jane Street I hoped to bump into Jane and make friends with her, but no-one ever took any notice of me. People were always busy, pushing past, looking stressed, unwilling to stop and talk to a Yorkie. Even when I wore my new, bright red harness with matching red human lead, no-one showed any interest in cuddling me.

Stewart came and went, as before, but when I took him for walkies further afield than Jane Street, things improved. Especially in an area called Greenwich Village. Here I attracted the kind of attention I deserve. Lots of very friendly men would look at me in my red harness as I walked Stewart on his red lead, and they would all want to get to know me and Stewart. I toyed with the notion that they were more interested in him than in me, but I know that's impossible.

Trips to Katia's office ceased. I spent more time in my new apartment, trying to find ways to avoid Gabriela's claws, which in such a confined space was quite a challenge. Then Katia stopped going to work. She had sold her business, apparently, which I find odd because whenever I do my business on the sidewalk no one ever offers money for it.

Then came a visit to the vet. A man in a white coat distracted me with a biscuit while he stuck a needle in me. The equivalent treatment for Gabriela involved ten times the normal amount of sedation, full protective clothing and a team of four assistants to hold her down. Katia told me the vet has a file on each of us. Mine just says 'Pitz' on the cover. Gabriela's has the initials V.V.B.C. after her name. This stands for 'Very Very Bad Cat'. Talk about an understatement.

With the inoculations inside me, I was invincible. I was rabies-proof and worm-proof. If any worms came at me, I would show no fear. I was also a cyber-dog. I had been fitted with a microchip. I had been enhanced with computer power and now I would reign supreme. As I trotted out the front door of the vet's building, intent on peeing at the foot of an interesting tree which I had spotted at the edge of the parking lot, I knew nothing could stop me. Suddenly I was scooped up into Katia's arms and deposited on the front seat of my car. I decided the tree could wait.

Then it happened again. With no warning, other than the boxes and the rolls of sticky tape and the packing and the removals men, the apartment in Jane Street was cleared out. Gabriela was hunted down and trapped and put into a secure cage amid much hissing and spitting. The cat wasn't too happy about it, either. I travelled in Katia's arms down to my waiting taxi. No sign of my own luxury car today. With just a few suitcases and the monster in its cage, we visited the airport.

Gabriela was checked in with the luggage on a flight to Paris. I hoped she might take a wrong turn and end up in some place where felines were on the menu.

Katia picked up a ticket for an economy class seat. I was to travel first class, however. Well, first class for a dog, which basically means Katia's lap. It's one of the perks of being so tiny. I don't need to travel in the cargo hold since I'm small enough to count as hand luggage.

I didn't recall having booked such a trip, but it seemed I was taking Katia to Paris. What a generous doggy I must have been. She would be very excited to visit such a romantic destination with me. I settled in for the journey, enjoying the sumptuous comfort of my top-of-the-range seat and revelling in the knowledge that Gabriela was shivering in her cage in a dark, unheated cargo hold. I knew how to travel.

We were in the air for forty-two hours (or about six hours if you're a human), and finally landed in the land of...the land of...well, the land of whatever France is famous for. Utterly daft-looking Poodles, I suppose. As soon as we had passed through immigration and into the baggage reclaim area, something happened that made my day. It was a dream come true.

The airline had mislaid Gabriela.

Mary

Yo, guess who? That's right! I was just thinking about how hungry I used to be when I was living in that Greek port. I lost so much weight that I looked two-dimensional. I worried about falling between the cracks in the pavement. Sometimes I was so weak that it was a struggle to walk. Almost anything I looked at became food. Pebbles would morph into potatoes. Sticks would sizzle like sausages, winking at me and daring me to eat them. But no matter how bad things were I never lost my enormous smile. It ran from one ear to the other. It made everything right. Even when people shooed me away from their homes or kicked me out of the grounds of the local church, I never lost that smile, never lost my belief that humans were good and decent, despite their outward appearances to the contrary. And I never lost my capacity to dream, to think that somewhere out across the blue ocean was a family who would take me in and love me.

Pooch

Who butted in just then? Come on, own up. I'm
going to count to ten. Actually, I'm not going to
count to ten because I can only count to one most of
the time, three or four on a good day, but I'm quite
proud of my ability; one is a pretty useful number. I
did consider becoming a mathematician, but it's
hard to hold the wand in my little paws. I wish I'd
mastered it, though, because I might have been able
to turn Gabriela into a newt, or, better still, a box of
chicken nuggets.

But why, I hear you ask (or I would do if I wasn't
so deaf these days) would I need to turn Gabriela
into a tasty meal if she had got lost in a Paris airport?
Well, sad to say, that story had a most unhappy
ending. After two hours of searching by the airline
staff, Gabriela was eventually located, still in her
crate, still breathing. Probably breathing fire,
knowing her.

Katia bundled the caged beast onto a trolley with
her suitcases, and with me marching alongside in my
bright red harness we walked through customs and
into the arrivals area. And this is where the day got
better again. There was good news to compensate for
Gabriela's safe arrival. Waiting for us was my second

favourite human: Stewart. It was almost as if he knew we would be there, almost as if he and Katia had planned this journey all along.

Stewart seemed very excited to see me, as indeed he should be, and he was moderately happy about welcoming Katia, too. He had driven there in a car that I hadn't seen before. It was a Renault Espace, and it wasn't as luxurious as the one I'd left behind in New York. It had a steering wheel on the wrong side, which meant that I was sat in what should have been the driving seat, kind of. Gabriela was shoved in the boot with the luggage where she belonged. No one spoke to her. Quite rightly. The Renault seemed to drive pretty well. In fact, I don't know why he never took that car to New York on his visits. Some humans are just odd. Anyhow, I decided this vehicle would suffice for my needs, especially considering that its vast size enabled a greater distance between me and the crated creature in the back.

We drove away from Paris, arriving by early afternoon at a farm in some remote part of France. There were chickens here. That was good. I was getting rather hungry by this stage. There were also other dogs here. That was not so good. I was going to have to let them know who was in charge. I hoped they understood English.

Katia and Stewart greeted the owner, a lady with auburn hair and a comforting smell of dog hair on her trousers and a hint of pee on her shoes, and we went for a tour of the place. Close to the farmhouse was a small prison for naughty animals. Concrete cells with metal doors. The prison cells had none of the comforts of home. I could see no sign of any of the essential things that a dog needs: no king-size bed with a memory foam mattress and feather pillows; no plush leather sofa; no cuddly toys to throw around at random. Those cells were bare and harsh. The only heat came from a red light bulb hanging from the ceiling. This must have been where only the world's most evil dogs and cats were sent for punishment, I decided. This was Alcatraz for animals. Colditz for cats. Something beginning with 'D' for dogs. No, I can't think of a prison beginning with 'D'. What about H Block for hounds? That sort of works, provided you understand the H Block reference. Which I don't.

I had no idea why I was being shown around this place. Then I remembered Gabriela, still in her crate in the back of the car. She was a Very, Very Bad Cat. This was her punishment. At last, justice was going to be served. I would finally be rid of this ferocious feline.

At first, this appeared to be precisely what was intended. The lady who owned the farm carried Gabriela from the car and put her into a high security cell, with nothing but a bed and a bowl of water. I was overjoyed. I waggled my imposing stump of a tail and danced with excitement. Gabriela was in jail and the planet was suddenly a safer place. She would serve her sentence in this bleak and lonely outpost of rural France. I imagined her getting tattoos on her face, taking up weightlifting, and getting into trouble for digging an escape tunnel. Such joyous daydreams!

We walked back to the farmhouse and I chased some chickens. I was on top of the world. It was the best day of my life. Katia and Stewart paid the farm lady some money, presumably a bribe to ensure that Gabriela would never be released. There were several other dogs in the farmhouse kitchen: a Spaniel with ears big enough to make a duvet out of; a Boxer who possessed no pugilistic skills whatsoever; and a Collie with a nose as long as my body. I pushed them about and made it clear that I was the top dog in this place, even though I had to crane my neck to look up at them. I played with their toys. I drank from their water bowls. There was nothing they could do. No-one would ever stand in my way.

The discussions between the humans continued for a while. They talked about stuff like rabies jabs and quarantine periods and how unfair the rabies laws were on the animals and I got bored and switched off. Finally, they stopped jabbering and we all returned to the prison cells again. Was it a last goodbye to Gabriela, I wondered? Were they giving me a chance to pee on the door to her cell, so that she would have a lasting reminder of my superior scent?

But we didn't go to Gabriela's cell. Katia picked me up and kissed me. Yuck. I wish she wouldn't do that – I don't know where she's been. Stewart tickled me behind the ears while Katia held me – I like that; ear tickles are the greatest – and then she put me into an empty cell with my bed and one toy. The metal door slammed shut. They walked away.

I barked. I had to let them know that they had made a mistake. They had inadvertently left me behind in a prison cell. Obviously they hadn't intended to do that, and they would realise their error in a moment and come back to set me free. I didn't belong there. I was special. I was not the kind of dog that lived a primitive, Spartan life.

No-one came.

I yapped. I howled. I cried. I coughed. I woofed. I yelped. I used the full range of my vocabulary, every word elucidated clearly at its maximum volume, but somehow Katia and Stewart didn't hear me. How could they forget me? I was the most important thing in their lives. I was probably the most important thing in the world, for that matter. Something must have gone badly wrong. But they would be back soon, I was sure. So I kept on barking. Barking had always been my primary weapon of control. There was a quality to my voice that inspired people to do my bidding. It had never failed me before, but this time they didn't return. My voice became hoarse. I grew tired. I was cold. I whimpered until I fell asleep. Abandoned. Rejected. Angry. I was too good for this. I deserved better.

The lady with the interesting smells brought me some food that evening. And I use the word 'food' in its loosest sense. It was a bowl of dog food. The final insult. Where was my scrambled egg with just a touch of ketchup and a side order of fillet steak and Béarnaise sauce? Where was my grilled chicken breast with pesto? Or my organic pasta twirls with melted Emmental cheese? I turned up my little nose at the mass-produced muck she had served me and sobbed myself to sleep, the emptiness in my stomach obscured by the pain in my heart.

The next morning, I awoke to find the nightmare had been real. Katia and Stewart had imprisoned me and then disowned me. I had become what I despised – a homeless, unloved and penniless mutt. How could I have let this happen? How had I lost my total control over my pet humans? I wondered if I had committed a crime, but that was impossible. I was a perfect dog. Katia had told me so, many times.

I wiped the crusty, dried tears from my face and surveyed my new surroundings. Concrete. Steel. The red lightbulb. And a bowl of stale dog food. Yummy. I wolfed it down, and instantly felt better. The food gave me the energy to begin barking again. The tactic had failed to work yesterday, but today it wouldn't let me down. Someone would rescue me. I was irresistible. I was adorable. I began yapping incessantly.

Just an hour later, someone arrived. Not the scented lady, but a young girl, barely three times my height. She smiled when she saw me. I smiled back and waggled my full inch of tail. She opened the door and let me out. I was free. My prison term had ended. I ran around looking for Katia and Stewart, but then I saw a chicken that needed chasing so I dealt with that first. After a good chase and a bit more barking I returned to the little girl so that she could cuddle me.

The dogs I had bullied yesterday in the kitchen joined us. I chased them around and reminded them that I was the boss. I also made it clear to them that from now on, access to the girl could only be arranged through me. Once they seemed to understand my elevated position in society, we chased a few chickens together, ran around pointlessly, threw some toys into the air and generally did all the things sophisticated and intelligent animals like to do. The girl joined in by throwing balls for me, and I responded by letting her retrieve them for me. I was having fun, but I wasn't truly happy. There was something missing in my life. A feeling of emptiness blighted the joy that I should have experienced that morning. For a moment I forgot what was causing it, and then it all came back to me. Katia. Stewart. My life of luxury and privilege. Where had it all gone?

I waddled to the edge of the farmhouse garden to have a poo. That helped. I always felt uplifted after one of those. The winter sun came out, warming the cold stone patio beside the house. I indulged in a spot of sunbathing. That felt good, too. I needed some colour. I snoozed. When I woke up it was late in the afternoon. Time to bully the other dogs, I decided, giving chase to the Boxer, and then snatching a tennis ball from the jaws of the Spaniel. The little girl played with me some more. I was starting to make the best of my bad situation. I was a winner. I would come out on top. I would take charge of her and her mother, as well as the dogs and the chickens and any other creatures who happened to be on this farm. I was born to be top dog, and I would fight to reclaim that status.

The girl picked me up and carried me back to the cell. She closed the door and left me there, shivering and alone. The second long night of incarceration was about to begin. There was nothing to do but bark repeatedly until my throat was worn down to the point where I could merely whisper. Where was Katia? Where was Stewart? And, for that matter, where was I?

The night passed slowly. I barely slept. I was consumed with disappointment and frustration. I couldn't help impatiently looking at the sky for signs of dawn, even though I had no-one to wake up anymore. When the sun finally came out of hiding, I was too tired to keep my eyes open. I dozed off into a deep sleep, from which I was rudely wrenched just moments later by the crowing of a cockerel. I had some serious chicken chasing to do today.

The games in the farmhouse garden were the same. I played. I barked. I chased. I relieved myself. Always over my shoulder I kept an eye out for my humans in case they came back for me, but once more I was let down.

Something odd happened that evening, however. Instead of being put back in my prison cell, I was invited into the farmhouse kitchen with the three other dogs. Somehow my bed had made it from my cell to the kitchen floor, and when darkness came and the woman and her daughter went to bed, they left me in the cosy kitchen with the Boxer, the Collie and the Spaniel. Could this mean the end of my jail term? Had I been released early in order to provide leadership and inspiration for these three losers sleeping next to me? I had no idea. All I knew was that I was out of that cold cell. I had a warm kitchen to sleep in. I had toys to play with. And I had other dogs to oppress.

Things were looking up, and just a few days later my situation improved further. A car arrived at the farm. It had a smell that I recognised. Katia and Stewart had come for me. They had realised their error in leaving me behind. They must have been driving for two or three days before remembering that they had accidentally left me in a French prison, and I pictured them screeching to a halt, turning around instantly and racing at full speed back to where they had left me. They would be full of remorse and bursting to apologise. I would be forgiving, I decided, but not before I'd made them feel guilty. Of course I would allow them back into my heart, but I would first play it cool. They needed to see that they had hurt me with their carelessness.

I resolved to appear indifferent to them. No smiling, no tail wagging, no jumping for joy. I would be an emotional blank canvas, as if I didn't even know them. Then they would understand what they had done to me.

I wet myself with excitement as soon as they stepped out of the car. Katia picked me up and told me I stank, and I licked her face to thank her for the compliment. My smile was wide enough to put Gabriela's head in. And then I remembered the cat monster. I hadn't seen her all week. She had remained in her cell where she belonged. But if Katia and Stewart were clever enough to come back for me, could they be stupid enough to collect Gabriela as well?

Happily not. Katia put me on her lap inside the car, and Stewart drove us away. Gabriela was just a bad memory, receding in the distance, never to be encountered again. My new life was just beginning. I wondered where I was taking us? I hadn't made any plans. It was all too sudden. Frankly I didn't care. I was with my family, and that was all that mattered. Details like where we were going to live could wait. It had been a long and difficult week on that farm prison. I could barely believe my ordeal was ended. I

fell asleep in Katia's arms and had an interesting
dream about sausages.

Mary

Yo, now that's a bizarre coincidence, because when I was living on the streets of Greece I used to dream about sausages, too. Except in those days, I had no idea what a sausage tasted like. All I knew was that they smelled good. I was surrounded by yummy odours back then. The restaurants in Greece made some wonderful dishes. Skopelos cheese pie was my favourite, even though I never got close to one. It was like a giant, curly sausage made from hot cheese and pastry. The aroma of one of those monster plates would waft for miles along the quayside, tickling my nose, teasing and tormenting me. I could have lived for a week from the calories in a Skopelos cheese pie, if only someone had been kind enough to give me one. But no-one ever did. I had to make do with nothing more than delicious smells. Every night I dined out on a three-course meal of air, filling my body with empty flavours, never letting go of the dream of a better life in which I would taste the actual foods from which those aromas came.

Pooch

Now that is bordering on dishonest. In fact, it's downright cheating. Butting in while I'm having a sausage dream is bang out of order; I had my guard lowered. But I'm back in the driving seat now, back to my story, which, of course, is the only one that matters.

When I woke up, Katia was still cradling me, as if I were a precious bundle of joy. Which I am. I remembered my task. I had to find us all a new home. We parked at a place called Versailles and walked up the steps to a grandiose palace. Seven hundred rooms. Two thousand windows. Sixty-seven staircases. One thousand chandeliers. And two thousand acres of doggy toilet. I peed against the base of a stone statue. The place was legally mine.

I needed a new home for my family. The Palace of Versailles, I decided, would do. I took Katia and Stewart on a tour of the gardens of our house. For some reason, they didn't want me to take them inside. Equally strange were the houseguests that were waiting for us. Hundreds of people were admiring my home. I assumed they were probably the neighbours, coming to welcome us. Some of them had brought their dogs with them. That would be the last time. In future, I would be the only dog here.

I needed a new home for my family.
The Palace of Versailles, I decided, would do.

I peed on a few more of the outer corners of the palace, thus cementing my legal claim and ensuring that I would own the property forever unless a *force majeure* (as the Poodles call it) should act to negate my title to the land, including, but not limited to, the scent wearing off after a few days, my pee being washed away by the rain, or me forgetting that I own it...

Own what? I can't remember what I was talking about. Usually I'm talking about myself, but I can't own myself, can I? That doesn't make sense, especially if my rights can wash away in a thunderstorm. Ah, yes. My new palace. We only spent a couple of hours there. For some reason, we left before our guests and returned to the car. We were probably going to a drapery shop to choose curtains for the two thousand windows.

When it became clear that we were never going back again, I decided the palace wasn't suitable for us after all. I would let some other dog claim it instead.

Stewart drove us a few miles to a campsite and parked next to a caravan. It had two windows, one door, and no chandeliers. There were no oil paintings, no bronze statues, no hanging tapestries. This place was so basic it wasn't even fit for a cat. Why had Stewart taken us there? But there was no time for such questions. Well, obviously, there was, because I just asked it, but I asked it in hindsight, if you think about it. Which I generally don't. Am I getting you confused? Never mind that. You're getting me confused. Stop it. I'm losing my thread again. All your fault! What was I saying? Cats and caravans. Yes. So, Katia picked me up and we walked to the street. A taxi stopped for us. Stewart said something to the driver using exotic and weird words that made even less sense than his usual language.

We climbed inside and as I dribbled on the window I deduced from the apparent infestation of Poodles in the area that I had taken my humans to Paris. Weren't they lucky? They didn't deserve me.

Our first stop was at a hill with a church on top. It was called Montmartre, and Katia enjoyed carrying me up the hundreds of steps to the white cathedral on the summit. After putting me on the ground for a quick pee (I mean me, not her, but don't always assume that), she put me in my special travel bag and slung me under her arm as we passed by the sign forbidding dogs from entering.

I like my travel bag. It's like a small sports bag, made from black fabric and with a flat base. There's a small and deliciously stinky blanket at the bottom, and I like to lie on it and look out at the world through the gauze window as Katia chauffeurs me around. I find it both relaxing and exciting. Relaxing, because I don't need to move my lazy legs at all, and exciting because when I go inside the bag it's usually because Katia wants to smuggle me into somewhere I'm not supposed to be. I felt like a spy on a secret and dangerous mission. There would be vicious hounds to overcome, refreshing bowls of water to drink (shaken, not stirred), and glamorous female dogs wanting to snuggle with me. Well, they would have a long wait. I don't share my bed with anyone.

Except for Katia and Stewart, and then only when I want to ensure they get a really bad night's sleep.

My spy fantasy evaporated when Katia opened the bag and held me in her arms so I could look at the view of Paris from the top of Sacré-Coeur. The ancient streets spread out like a map below us. In the centre of the maze of roads and buildings was a metal tower, far taller than anything else in the city. It looked like a giant chew. I wanted it.

But first there were more cathedrals for me to be smuggled into. I breezed past security into Notre Dame and courageously kept the hunchback at bay from within my travel bag. I achieved a similar success in St Sulpice, when I surreptitiously sniffed the odours of a dozen American tourists who were doing something called a 'Da Vinci Code Trail'. Feeling much enlightened by my afternoon of high culture and history, I was prepared for the ultimate cultural experience: the Louvre museum. It was here that I encountered an insurmountable hurdle.

An X-ray scanner. All visitors' bags had to be X-rayed at the entrance. There was no way to smuggle me in undetected. Katia and Stewart must have been disappointed that I wouldn't get a chance to pee on the Mona Lisa, but I coped well. I had already seen many things that I wasn't supposed to see and peed in lots of places where I should have kept my legs crossed. It had been a great day. I had shown my pet humans a good time. Now I wanted to take them out to dinner.

At the Louvre museum there was no way to smuggle me in undetected. Katia and Stewart must have been disappointed that I wouldn't get a chance to pee on the Mona Lisa.

I found them a traditional Parisian restaurant, and Katia hid me in the bag once again as we were shown to a table. Half way through the meal she opened the gauze window so that I could see what was going on. I behaved myself, staying seated and just looking around. My excellent behaviour and highly tuned spying skills ensured that I could see without being seen. The waiter certainly didn't notice me, although he did bring me delicious doggy biscuits on several occasions.

By this time it had got dark. We walked a little and found a street named Avenue de New York. I peed against the sign. It reminded me of my long-lost home across the ocean. I wondered how the house by the Hudson was doing. Would it become infested with cats without me there to protect it? And what about our current homeless predicament? I still hadn't found us somewhere to sleep. In the taxi back to the campsite, I imagined we might drive into the night, perhaps not stopping until we had found the ideal home, but there was to be no more travelling that night. Stewart opened the door to the caravan and Katia carried me inside. I was so insulted by having to spend a night in that slum accommodation that I didn't know whether to pee and poo inside it or out. In the end I did neither, falling contentedly asleep in the warm valley that the duvet made between Stewart's legs.

We found a street named Avenue de New York.
I peed against the sign.

Waking up in a caravan – can you imagine anything less suitable for a pedigree like me? The shame of it! There was nowhere on the planet I was less keen to spend another night, apart from my prison cell on the farm, the horrific memories of which were already starting to fade. So, after an odd night in that aluminium box on wheels, I made Stewart and Katia drive me away to somewhere better. Perhaps we could give that palace at Versailles a second go? I think we made a poor choice when we walked away from that. My humans would see things my way and take me back there.

But they didn't do that. They took me somewhere even worse than the caravan. I thought humans had the capability to learn from their mistakes, but not my two. They inadvertently drove back to the farm and accidentally put me in the prison compound once again. Then they drove away, without realising they had left me behind. No amount of barking could bring them back. The Boxer, the Collie and the Spaniel all looked at me as if they were pleased to see me. That made me particularly cross. They should have been horrified at my abandonment; they should have shown disappointment in their faces, but all they did was wag their tails and sniff my behind, gleaning from the aromas therein the story of all the places I had visited in Paris. A dog doesn't need to read Bill Bryson: one sniff and the whole travel adventure unravels before them.

These dogs were taking liberties with my smells. I needed to remind them that I was the boss. I resolved to do so with an impressive, jaw-dropping display of my virility and masculinity. So I picked up a battered cuddly toy in my mouth and threw it several inches across the farmyard. I had staked my claim as ruler and there was nothing they could do about it.

As it turned out, none of them had been watching, so I did it again. And again. By this point I couldn't remember why I was throwing the toy around, but it seemed like a fun thing to be doing, so I carried on until one of the bigger dogs took it from me and I walked off to have a sulk.

I allowed the woman who looked after the animals at the farm to let me sleep in the kitchen that night. It was better than going back to the cell, but there was no escaping the stark reality that my humans had forgotten me. I was ready to sink into a deep depression. And then something happened that cheered me up. I remembered that Gabriela was still in her cold and lonely cell. I waggled my tail as I nodded off. Life wasn't all bad.

The next weekend, Katia and Stewart realised the error of their ways and returned for me. But after two days living with them in a small cottage just a few miles away, they put me back in the prison compound and drove off again. These weekend visits became the norm. Every time they came I was elated to see them, and every time they left me behind I was devastated, but probably not as devastated as they must have been each time they realised that they had forgotten me.

And so winter rolled into spring, the sunbathing opportunities grew longer, the weekend visits continued, and that seemed to be the best my life could hope for. It was far less than I deserved. I needed to focus. I needed to find a way to put things right. At the end of Katia and Stewart's next visit, I would refuse to be left behind. I would make them take me somewhere else. I didn't know where exactly, but I had a vision in my little mind of a house and a garden big enough for all of us. It couldn't be hard to find.

At the end of the week they arrived and plonked me in the front seat of the car, as usual. This time, though, they took longer to drive away. There were discussions with the farm lady. There were things being put in the back of the car. Things I didn't like the smell of. Things that made me uneasy.

As the journey began, those smells began to take shape in my nose. I decoded the assembled whiffs. It wasn't good. I could smell something sinister. I could smell Gabriela.

What was the point of bringing this convicted animal with us, I wondered? There was only one logical explanation. She was being transferred to another prison. Hopefully something with higher security and a bed made from broken glass and old syringes. I pictured her new cell, heated with ice cubes, crawling with cockroaches. I realised my imagination was straying too far. Even Gabriela didn't deserve that. She deserved scorpions, instead.

The next stop was at a vet's. This made me happy. It was a chance to explain to a professional medical person the problems I had been experiencing with my humans. How they regularly forgot all about me. How they abandoned me to a life on a farm where I was fed dog food as if I were some unimportant, regular hound. The vet might have a cure for Katia and Stewart's amnesia. Some kind of injection in their bottoms, perhaps?

But when I was lifted onto the examination table, my plan fell apart. As always, I went all gooey at the hands of the vet. I like to be fussed about. I adore being the centre of attention where I belong, and when a vet starts examining me I forget about everything else and simply relish every moment of it.

Mary

Yo! I remember hearing about vets when I was living under my wheelie bin, but I didn't believe in them. Vets, I mean, not wheelie bins. Vets were mythical beings, like unicorns or mermaids. When other dogs talked about these mysterious humans with healing powers, I rolled my eye and sighed. It couldn't be true. No one had ever healed my ailments, after all, and I had plenty of medical problems back then. There were ticks sucking my blood. There were tapeworms in my stomach, eating what little food came their way. I had my eye injury, and I had all the scars from the abuse and violence I had already experienced in my young life. I wanted to believe in vets, but they just seemed too good to be true. They would have to be magicians to be able to make our medical problems go away. A person who could stop pain instead of inflicting it? Surely that was impossible. A human who could soothe my discomfort instead of making it worse? It was stretching credulity too far. If vets really existed, they would have healed me. And, in any case, how could such wonderful human beings walk on the same planet as the people who threw sticks and stones at me and left me to starve?

Vets were not the only myths circulating amongst the stray community. Some strays talked about the way other dogs lived. They invented stories of dogs who were fed every day, groomed and cuddled, loved and appreciated, walked and played with. These make-believe dogs were fixed up by equally fanciful vets whenever there was something wrong with them. In some legends, there was talk of dogs who slept indoors on soft beds. I had never heard anything so preposterous. I didn't believe these fairy stories; they were too far removed from my life to sound realistic. And even if there was such a thing as a dog who slept in a soft bed, or such a thing as a vet, I didn't think I would ever get to meet one. I just assumed I would always live under a bin, and that my ailments would be with me forever, and that I should just get on with life as best I could.

Pooch

If I wasn't so small that I could fit in your mouth, Homeless Mary, and still give you room to brush your teeth, I'd say horrid things directly to your face and make you cry. But I'm better than that. Besides, you've never had your teeth manicured and polished like me. And I'm not the sort to intimidate other dogs. Unless they're called Mary and grew up on the mean streets of Greece. So just stay out of my way and, more importantly, stay out of my story. You'll get a proper mention later on. I'll make sure your side of the story is told in a fair and balanced way. Just wait for the impartially-written chapter where I describe how my life was ruined by your arrival. In that chapter I'll talk about how you crashed into my life and spoiled things for me, how I hated every second spent with you, and how unfair and rubbish the situation became. But I don't want to spoil the surprise by telling the readers that you're destined to end up squatting in my home and how awful I felt about having you there. Only an idiot would reveal crucial future developments in the plot so soon in the book.

Right, back to the plot. There I was, being fussed over by a French vet, which I love because it means

I'm the centre of attention where I belong, before waiting in the car while Gabriela almost instigated a world war in her attempt to avoid having the same experience. If she hated vets so much, why did the stupid cat bother to be born an animal in the first place? She never thought things through, that was her problem. Well, one of them. When the blood and collateral damage from the cat's veterinary visit was cleaned up, we set off for our destination that evening: the same cottage in which we had stayed previously on Katia and Stewart's weekend visits with me. I wondered briefly if this was our new permanent home, but it didn't smell right. It didn't have the furniture and the paintings and the books that combined to create the unique flavour that I recognised as home. It also lacked my own special contribution to its collection of odours, but that was something I resolved to work on with immediate effect.

I peed on the kitchen rug and blamed Gabriela for it, even though she was still incarcerated in her travel cage.

I rubbed my bottom along the floor, hoping to create a pattern of straight lines. Gabriela made me do it, I said.

I dribbled on the cushions that were scattered across the sofa. Definitely Gabriela's fault.

But my efforts were wasted. Before lunchtime the next day we had packed our things and were driving through the country lanes of France once again. Was this to be another journey back to the prison farm? After two hours, the answer became clear. We were not anywhere near the prison. Stewart had bought an enormous yacht and we were going sailing.

We got in line with the hundreds of cars who were joining us on this private cruise. Presumably they were guests of ours. I didn't like the look of them. Especially the ones with dogs in their cars. Slowly we drove inside the belly of the ship. The vessel was enormous. I was very impressed that my humans had bought it, and had probably done so just for my benefit. I sat and waited to be taken to my first-class cabin. Katia and Stewart got out of the car and closed the door. Stewart reached back in and disabled the alarm before locking me inside. They had forgotten about me yet again. I wished I hadn't forgotten to mention their amnesia to the vet.

I made myself comfortable in the warm driving seat, and settled down for the voyage. I couldn't see Gabriela, but I could hear her spitting and fuming from within her cage in the back. I hoped her noises might attract the attention of a shark or a giant squid, and I waited for pointy teeth or slimy tentacles to reach in and try to drag the feline beast to the bottom of the sea. Although, quite frankly, I suspected that even an oversized marine predator would swim away crying for its mummy after an encounter with Gabriela.

Soon I was asleep, dreaming of scrambled egg. By the time I had licked the plate clean, the car doors opened and I woke up. At least I had been able to finish the imaginary egg before being disturbed. There's nothing worse than dreaming of food and not having enough sleep time to eat it all and then waking up hungry. I opened my eyes and sat up. The ship was no longer moving. Our cruise was over and Stewart drove us onto dry land. We had arrived in a strange country, a rather damp and cloudy island sandwiched between the North Sea and the Atlantic Ocean. Hmm, sandwiches. Ham sandwiches are the best, in case you were wondering. Anyway, after a brief stop to show off my pet passport to an admiring policeman, we drove off on the wrong side of the road. I wasn't too worried about that, however, because everyone else also drove on the wrong side, so I supposed it cancelled out any danger. Stewart said the country was called England, and I wasn't impressed. It didn't seem sunny enough for me.

Our destination was a place called Chichester – in particular, a house that had been built two hundred and fifty years ago. This, it seemed, was to be our home.

Two hundred and fifty years old? Talk about cheapskates! Why couldn't I have a new one? And the disappointments didn't end there. The house had stairs. Lots of them. And very little in between. But it wasn't until Katia opened the back door for me that I beheld the final insult: the garden was tiny. It wasn't even a garden. It was a courtyard, an area smaller than a human bathroom, penned in by steep brick walls. There was no lawn and no sun.

This simply would not do. I decided to pack my bags and head back to France. At least the sun shone there. But then Katia produced a present for me: a new squeaky ball. I frothed with excitement as I played with this marvellous new toy until the novelty wore off and I got bored with it, which was about thirty seconds later. By then I had forgotten about my plan to return to France, and settled into my job of decoding the various sniffs to be found throughout this peculiar Georgian townhouse. Putting two centuries of smells into some kind of order was a challenge that I didn't relish. So I did what I always do when faced with something that could tax my brain: I gave up and sat on Katia's lap while Stewart unloaded the car.

Watching him carrying heavy luggage soon wore me out. I closed my eyes and drifted away and dreamed about licking dirty plates clean. I'm good at that. Good enough to get paid, I reckon. Obviously, I would never have to get a job for two reasons: one, because I'm too important and special and cuddly, and seven, because I'm completely and utterly useless. But if I ever lowered myself to such a status, I think my ideal position would be in the kitchen of a restaurant, licking the dirty plates as they came back from the tables until they were spotless and ready to use again.

It took a while to adjust to life in England. Everyone spoke with a peculiar accent. Rather like Stewart, in fact. Half the time I didn't know what they were talking about. Actually, all of the time, since I'm always too wrapped up in my own little world to pay attention to anyone else. I got to know my new grandparents, and would often spend fun-filled weekends with them in their house, which I decided was my holiday home. I would play with their toys, sit on their laps, and make full use of their garden facilities. Being a generous dog, I let them stay in my holiday home even when I wasn't with them.

Gabriela still skulked around the house. She had been released from prison early, but she showed no sign of gratitude or contrition, whatever they are. In such a small space, I was hardly any better off than I had been in the apartment in Jane Street, New York. I missed my garden by the Hudson. I missed running around stupidly and chasing innocent ducklings randomly. The house in Chichester was simply inadequate for the requirements of a dog such as me. It was time to start house hunting.

Oddly enough, Katia and Stewart seemed to have the same idea. They often went out without me, looking at properties, coming home with brochures, talking about the advantages of one house over the next. They had meetings with banks, lawyers, and accountants. This went on for weeks, which I found most bizarre and frustrating. Why didn't they just find a place they liked and pee on it? Job done. Humans are weird.

It took about six months before we moved out of that little house. By then Katia's furniture had arrived in a container from America, and there was absolutely no room left anywhere. We had to move somewhere bigger. But this time there was no removal truck. The move happened slowly, one car load at a time, beginning with the most important item in the house. Me.

The journey to my next home lasted twenty minutes. We were no longer in Chichester. In fact, we were no longer in England, it seemed. We had crossed a bridge onto a little island called Hayling. I could smell the classic odours of the sea: salt water, gulls, fish and chips. Were we going to live on a boat? I was so excited with anticipation that I almost stayed awake.

The final bend in the route woke me up. I stood up on Katia's lap in the passenger seat, dug my feet uncomfortably (for her, I mean – don't worry!) into her thighs, and prepared myself for the view.

And there it was. My new home, in all its magnificence. My English castle.

Well, they say an English dog's home is his castle. Don't they? Therefore, it was a castle. OK, it was built in the early seventies, and the top floor was made from wood and so probably wouldn't stand up to sustained cannon fire from an army of invading cats, but for a little pooch like me it was a veritable fortress. There were several outdoor bathrooms in the front garden: a large oak tree in the centre of it, and rows of Leyland cypress trees around the borders. Katia put me on the driveway so I could explore. I immediately ran to the back garden to check out the pee-pee facilities. I found lawns and more Leyland cypresses; in fact, there were more trees than I could shake a leg at. This was looking good. I even had my own private swimming pool.

I ran up the back steps and into the house. It had rooms. I like rooms. And in those rooms, there were plush seventies curtains in wondrous shades of brown and orange. There were varnished pine ceilings, like a giant sauna. There were dark green carpet tiles on the kitchen floor, stained with thirty years of dropped food; the sniffs to be had in there would keep me busy for hours. The house was split between two floors on one side, and another floor half way between the two on the other. A bit like a normal house with a bungalow stuck on the side. Nothing in there had been touched since the seventies. Stewart said it felt like a set for *The Good Life*, only without so many chickens. I had no idea what he meant by that, but then I never had a clue what he was on about, anyway. I carried on exploring and found an indoor cellar and an outdoor cellar, two living rooms, four bedrooms, and some bathrooms for the humans to use (they were a bit funny about using my own bathroom in the garden – I don't know why).

And the best thing about my new castle? It was as big as the old house by the Hudson. That meant I would have space to keep away from the cat, and she would be able to keep away from me. Sure, the place needed some work doing to it – just a few hundred grand (which, I have been assured, is a lot of money, whatever that is) would bring it up to the kind of specification that would be appropriate for me. Katia and Stewart started immediately. Actually, Katia started the refurbishment while Stewart went to work each day. One evening he came home to find the pine ceiling from the living room was now a pile of planks on the floor. Katia looked at him with a crowbar in her hand and a guilty look on her face. At least she didn't blame it on me.

The upgrade took years: carpets up, skirting boards ripped out, lights replaced, bathrooms torn out and thrown into skips. The makeover of my castle left it with new wiring, new heating, new wall coverings, new doors, new windows, new cupboards, new kitchen, new insulation, new colours, new everything. They turned the second living room into a cinema so that I could fall asleep on Katia's lap while she watched movies on a nine-foot screen. They turned the garage into an office so that Stewart could work from home with Katia. Then they built a log cabin behind the garage so that Stewart could work from home, but away from Katia. They put a log burner in the living room to keep me cosy in winter. They remodelled the back garden to make the lawn perfectly flat so that I could play without the inconvenience of going uphill at all. They planted palm trees and hundreds of other plants for me to water. My castle became magnificent. People thought it was brand new. That was the kind of admiration I craved. From my palace, I could look down upon the lowly dogs in the neighbourhood. They didn't have their own cinema. They didn't have their own pool or their own palm tree-themed outdoor bathroom.

If you think life was finally perfect for me, just wait. The news gets even better. Because while all these improvement works were happening, Gabriela was getting old. She was always a few years older than me, and I never seemed to catch up with her no matter how many birthdays I had. As the castle renovation neared completion, she was about sixteen or seventeen. In cat years, that made her old enough to remember when Shirley Temple was a big box office draw. And she started getting sick. Her aggression subsided slightly. She almost became sweet. At times, I nearly felt sorry for her, but not quite. She was still a cat, and she didn't deserve to share my home. Anyway, a brave vet examined her and gave her some medicine to take, but the prognosis was not good (which means it was very good indeed). She was dying. The treatment resulted in no improvement, and so Katia and Stewart took Gabriela to the vet for a second time.

I waited at home while this visit was going on. Someone had to guard the castle, after all. An hour later, Katia and Stewart returned with Gabriela still in her travel crate. The cat monster was uncharacteristically quiet. I thought no more of it until Stewart went into the garden, grabbed a shovel and started digging a hole. A second swimming pool, perhaps, something designed just for me, since the other pool was a little deep for my four inch legs? But it wasn't another swimming pool. Katia brought Gabriela to him wrapped in a blanket, and he put her in the hole and started shovelling soil over the beast (I'm still talking about Gabriela, not Katia) until she was completely covered up.

I couldn't believe what I was seeing. For a moment, it made me very angry. Why hadn't he done this years ago, I wondered? If burying the cat had always been an option, it should have happened right at the start, back when we were still living in America. Why make me suffer all those years of co-habitation first?

I never did find out if Gabriela was actually dead when they put her in that hole. I suppose she might have put up more resistance if she had been alive, but just to be on the safe side I inspected the site every day in case she was digging her way out. If that ever happened, I had a plan. I would drag my toys there so that the combined weight of all those squeaky ducks and furry bears would keep her in her place. My careful surveillance of the site proved to be unnecessary, however. Gabriela remained under the soil.

So that was the end of Gabriela. I hope I've portrayed her demise in a sensitive and appropriate way. I hope my account of her final days has been moving. I was genuinely moved by her funeral. And by moved, of course, I mean I was jumping for joy. That's the kind of movement I experienced, and it went on for weeks.

She had gone from my house. Gone from my life. The only thorn in my side had been removed, and now I had everything a little dog could wish for: a luxury home with the undivided attention of my two devoted human pets. I had made it. I was on top of the world.

And then they went sailing.

It seemed harmless enough. We were living on an island, after all, so why not learn to sail? It started with a week's course on a yacht in the Solent. While I stayed with my grandparents, Katia and Stewart went to sea to learn how to pull ropes and be shouted at. They also learned how to make tea in the galley kitchen and how to lose their expensive sunglasses overboard. Stewart, apparently, excelled in that department. They came back a week later stinking of salt water and holding certificates in their hands. That's where they should have left it, and all would have been well. But they were only qualified as 'competent crew' –they wanted more. They wanted to be able to skipper their own boat, even though they didn't have one.

Another year passed. I remained in blissful ignorance of what was to come. I enjoyed my luxury and my power and my status. I was in command of my own little universe. I even managed to persuade Stewart to upgrade his car from the Espace to a Lexus, similar to the one I had been used to in America. At first he complained about how much additional money it would cost him – a peculiar concept that meant nothing to me – before he eventually granted my modest wish. I would take him and Katia for drives to the beaches of Hayling Island, and very soon the plush carpets of his new car bore the distinctive pawprints of wet sand and the irresistible aroma of damp dog.

It was a fabulous time, but my humans kept talking about another sailing course. This would mean abandoning me for another week – how anyone could conceive of such actions I have no idea. And if that wasn't bad enough, this time they wanted to do it somewhere warmer than the Solent. They wanted to take their next sailing course in Greece.

Of course, I tried to stop them, but my pleading was misinterpreted as a barking demand for a biscuit, and when that yummy biscuit was in my mouth I then forgot all about what I was trying to tell them. So I was bundled off to my holiday home for a couple of weeks bossing my grandparents about and making them treat me like a prince while Katia and Stewart went to the airport, flying out to an island called Skiathos, from where they would sail to ports such as Skopelos and Orei.

It sounded ghastly.

Mary

Yo! My goodness, I do feel I need to apologise, dearest and most gorgeous reader. I've been rabbiting on about my life in Greece as if I was really unhappy there. Please don't get the wrong impression. Yes, at times I was lonely and hungry and sick and cold and wet and injured. And there were also the times when I was verbally and physically abused... and the times when I was frightened and desperate and weak... but there were certain things that I always carried around with me. These things never left me, even throughout my darkest days. What were these things? You should know by now! It's not as if I had anything physical to carry, after all. I'm talking about my smile and my hopes and my dreams. And I always saved my biggest smile for the sailors who arrived in my port. They weren't always interested in me, but some of them returned a smile that was almost as big as my own, and that simple interaction would make my heart flutter. One little act of kindness or generosity would feed my soul for days. These small highlights in my life kept me going, and boy am I glad I kept going, because eventually some rather special people arrived in Orei, people who were going to change my life.

The day started quietly. It was the height of summer and the sun glared down onto the concrete of the quayside, burning the pads of my paws as I walked. I hadn't eaten for a couple of days, other than salad. And by salad, of course, I mean grass and weeds, usually with a dressing of... well, it's probably best not to know. I knew the hunger pangs would subside when I lay in the sun, so I decided to spend the day basking in the thick, warm air next to my wheelie bin in the harbour, waiting for sleep to take away the pain altogether.

That plan was completely turned on its head when a yacht arrived. The people on board were shouting at each other and trying their best not to hit the other boats as they reversed their yacht against the dock, right next to where I was sunbathing. Their attempts to avoid denting the neighbouring vessels were largely unsuccessful, and I spent a few minutes being mildly amused by the spectacle of their ineptitude. Eventually the boat was secured, the shouting stopped, and a rather unsafe and wobbly-looking plank was placed between the yacht and the quayside. Five humans cautiously walked across the plank to join me next to the bin. I stretched, waggled my tail and smiled feebly at them. They smiled back. I was on Cloud Nine.

'Oh look, a stray dog,' said one of them.

I hadn't eaten for a couple of days, other than salad.
And by salad, of course, I mean grass and weeds.

'The poor thing only has one eye,' said another.

Not that I understood a word they said, of course, because I'm Greek and they spoke a different language. It was called English and it sounded strange and exotic to me. But body language is international, and I could read the friendliness in their faces. They walked off to get some lunch and, having nothing better to do, I decided to follow them. I kept a respectful distance, and I don't think they even noticed me.

They settled themselves at a table in one of the many outdoor restaurants that overlooked the harbour. I waited until they had sat down before finding a spot for myself on the ground a couple of metres away. I stretched out and sunbathed contentedly.

'Isn't that the same stray dog we just saw?' one of them said. 'Look, it's the one-eyed dog from the port.

'Look, it's the one-eyed dog from the port.'

I didn't know what they were talking about, but I grinned at them and returned to my sunbathing.

They ate their lavish meal, occasionally looking at me and talking about me. None of their feast made its way towards my dry mouth, and that was fine. I didn't expect anything. The food on the table belonged to the humans, not to me. I knew my place. I belonged on the ground, suffering a silent hunger. I knew better than to beg for scraps.

When their lunch was finished, I trotted after them back to the boat. Here my patience was rewarded by the arrival of a bowl of food and another of water, which they placed on the dock for me just behind their boat. It seemed they had pocketed part of their meal and kept it to give to me. I wetted my mouth with a little aperitif, then sniffed the contents of the food bowl. Lumps of cheese and some scraps of ham. It tasted divine. A split second later the entire contents of the bowl entered the cavern of my stomach. The arrival of the food echoed amid the emptiness of my insides. These were lovely people. My instinct was right. I drank the rest of the water, then lay on the quayside with a grin that was large enough to trap a bird while they smiled back at me from the yacht.

I dozed for a few minutes, then awoke to the sound of the humans talking. I yawned and stretched. They were crossing the rickety passerelle towards me. I guessed they were about to walk back into town. I stood up and walked behind them, enjoying the novel sensation of having a meal inside me, but when they reached the crowded street where the waterside restaurants were located, I lost sight of them. With just the one eye it's harder to keep track of where people are, and I twisted my head in confusion at the mass of legs and feet moving along the pavement. It had been fun while it lasted. Following them around had provided me with a little entertainment and distraction, and now it was over. Perhaps I would see them later when they returned to the yacht, or perhaps I would never see them again. I was prepared for that.

Then I heard a woman's voice.

'Mary!'

It came from the other side of the bustling street. I had never heard the name Mary before; I didn't know what it meant, but something deep within me told me that it was meant for me. I ran in the direction of the voice and saw the group of humans who had just fed me. I waggled my tail and smiled at them. They seemed pleased.

'See,' said the woman to the others, 'I told you her name was Mary.'

'How did you know?' asked one of them.

'Because she told me.'

'What, she said "hello, my name is Mary?"'

'Don't be daft. I just sensed it.'

I was Mary. I had a name. I wasn't just a dog. I wasn't
just a nuisance stray, an anonymous street hound. I
was Mary.
I was somebody.

I sensed it, too. I was Mary. I had a name. I wasn't
just a dog. I wasn't just a nuisance stray, an
anonymous street hound. I was Mary. I was

somebody. Mary. Mary. Mary. The word was like music. I loved it. Mary. I said it to myself over and over. I was bursting with pride. None of the other street dogs in Orei had names. I was Mary. They were going to be so jealous. In the land of the unnamed dogs, the one-eyed mongrel would be queen. I had never felt so important.

Pooch

Right. If you're feeling emotional about Mary getting a name, stop it now. Put those tissues away. Don't be so soppy. Just because a dog doesn't have a name is no reason to feel gooey about it. Some of my favourite fluffy toys don't have names and if I suddenly started calling them Norman or Roger or Engelbert that's hardly a reason to crack open the champagne. With or without names, I still throw my toys around the room and try to rip their heads off (though my playful attempts at beheading them always end without success because for some reason my jaws lack the power and grip that a dog of my status ought to possess). Getting a name is nothing to be proud of. And 'Mary' is hardly as posh as all the names I get called: 'Pitz', 'Pooch' and 'that stupid dog'.

Mary

I trotted merrily around Orei all afternoon, often losing track of the humans who had named me, but always listening on the wind for that magic word to appear. Mary. I heard it again and ran to the woman's side. She laughed and patted my head.

'It's like she's our dog,' the woman said.

'It's really spooky. Wherever we are, we just have to shout "Mary" and she arrives from nowhere,' said another.

I waggled my tail again at the mention of my name. They started to walk away and I followed them a little closer than normal, deep in my private fantasy that I really was their dog. I indulged my imagination and pretended that they really would be my humans and let me into their family. I wondered what it would be like to live with them. Perhaps they would let me have a bowl of Skopelos cheese pie every week? I could fend for myself with a diet of insects and scraps and grass for most of the time, but to have a guaranteed meal once a week would be heavenly. Perhaps they would give me clean water every now and then, too. I didn't mind the taste of puddle water, but sometimes I would go thirsty in the long days of summer. They probably lived in a house somewhere, and maybe they would let me have the privilege of sleeping on their driveway, and perhaps on their doorstep when it rained.

Who was I kidding? I knew this could never happen. I had been born on the streets and within a year or so I would die there. All of the dogs around me were young. I had never seen a dog older than two years. My life was destined to be brief and tough, but I would love everyone I met on this short journey and try to make the best of things. It would be a lonely existence – no person or animal stayed with me for long – but that wouldn't suppress my positive disposition. Right now, I was with people who seemed to care about me, and that was enough. Right now, I was happy. Right now, I was Mary.

When they returned to their yacht that evening I lay on the quayside in front of them and remained there until the skies darkened and a thunderstorm arrived. The humans retreated into their yacht and sealed the hatches. I wished I could go with them and shelter from the storm in their affectionate company, but I knew my place was on the quayside, not on the boat, and besides I was terrified of walking across the wobbly passerelle. As the lightning split the sky apart and the rain lashed mercilessly across the land and sea, I retreated as far as possible beneath the wheelie bin and shivered as I waited for the long, cold night to end.

The morning sun quickly dried all trace of the floods of rainwater that had drenched me the night before. There was no more food in the bowl that the humans had put out for me, so I went rummaging for breakfast in town. Caterpillars. Dead flies. The back half of a mouse. No sign of the front half but, as it turned out, I needn't have bothered looking, because back at the quayside by the yacht I found the bowl had been filled with sliced salami and biscuits. Seconds later the meal was inside me, once again granting me the unfamiliar yet wondrously pleasing sensation of having eaten as much food as my body needed.

Pooch

Talking of food, where's my supper? It's time for my third meal of the day. I usually get my home-cooked, organic scrambled egg by now, mixed with some expensive artisan cheeses and a little smoked salmon. This delay is inexcusable. I'll have to have a word with my catering staff. I refuse to be kept waiting and treated like some kind of animal.

While I wait for my overdue meal I'll talk a little more about me. I'm great. You probably know that already. I'm sure my awesomeness shines through in every word I write. There has probably never been a more amazing, a more wonderful, or a more modest dog in the history of this planet. And that is why the things that were soon to happen to me in this story are so grossly unfair and unjust.

Mary

As I sunbathed contentedly after my salami and biscuits, the humans appeared on the deck of the boat and started to do things with ropes. I had seen this kind of behaviour before. It was usually a preface to their departure. One of them took some photos of me as I sat alone on the concrete of the quayside, then they hauled the passerelle back onto the yacht, started the engine, and slipped away.

'Bye Mary!' they shouted. I still had my name, but I no longer had my humans, and without them the name was a hollow sound. Meaningless. They were gone. I would never see them again. I closed my eye and felt tears leak onto both sides of my face. I couldn't see with both eyes, but I could still cry with them.

Pooch

Before things got bad, they got better. Katia and Stewart returned from their sailing holiday and collected me from the holiday home that I generously shared with my grandparents. They were talking about their adventures at sea and they kept going on about some disgusting and deformed vagrant mongrel called Mary. I always try to filter out any conversations that are not about me, but they blabbered on about Mary so much that it was impossible to ignore. I tried to distract them from their irrelevant reminiscences by being generally cute and adorable, which obviously comes completely naturally to me, but for once it wasn't working. My charms were failing. This mystery hound had crept into their minds and wouldn't leave. They talked about this dog for months. I sensed this could turn into a significant problem, but something else turned up in the meantime that seemed to offer a brief reprieve.

One morning I was taken to the vet so that he could admire my incredible physique. He wrote some complimentary comments in my pet passport, and the next day I was placed in the back of Stewart's car along with bags of stuff. With Stewart driving and Katia in the front seat, we began a journey. I didn't know where I was taking them, and I decided to go with the flow and see where we ended up. The car drove onto a train and went through a long tunnel, and when we emerged at the other end we were in a place that smelled suspiciously familiar. Baguettes. Snails. Poodles. Was I to return to the hellhole site of my French incarceration? Was this to be the end of my perfect existence, the final day of my living in fully justified and deserved luxury and pampering?

We continued driving. Far longer than it would have taken to return to that animal prison. The autumn sun grew stronger. The temperature increased a little. We spent the night in a hotel and continued heading south the next day. There was another border. We reached a strange land I had not encountered before. It smelled different to France. The aroma was hard to define. I suppose it was just a bit more fishy. We parked the car and walked to a little house. I peed on the front step. It now belonged to me. Stewart opened the front door to let me in. I ran straight to the back door, demanding to inspect the back garden. Katia opened the door and I ran onto the terrace, down to the garden, then skidded to a halt in shock. At the end of the little garden was an ocean. A vast expanse of sea water, right there in front of me. There were boats on the sea, and in the far distance I could spy land: another country, just sitting there across the ocean. Then I spotted a dog being taken for a walk on the shore of that remote country, and I barked at it. The foreign dog looked at me briefly, then peed against a tree.

The sun shone brightly here. It was a welcome reprieve from the grey skies of England. I liked this waterside house. My toys and bed arrived in the living room and I felt at home with my own whiffs. This was my new holiday home in the sun, and it was great. It was precisely what a dog like me deserved. I subsequently learned that the water behind the house was a canal, not an ocean, but it led directly to the Mediterranean Sea and I spent hours each day watching the boats come and go. Some of the boats had dogs on board.

I decided I also deserved a boat.

A day or two later, my vessel arrived. It was beautiful. Exciting. Huge. Stewart pumped it up in just five minutes, stuck an electric outboard motor on the back, connected it to a car battery, and off we went to explore the canals. I sat at the front of the boat, directing where to go. This seemed appropriate as I had a considerable degree of nautical experience, having once jumped into a river from which I had to be rescued by Katia. I explored the canals and the marina, marvelled at the waterside homes and the yachts, and barked at any dogs who had the impertinence to look at me from their gardens.

There was an immaculate beach just a few minutes from the house, and slightly further away was another beach, somewhat less immaculate, where dogs were permitted. This place was perfection. My life was perfection. I had a fabulous home in England, plus the weekend holiday home with my grandparents, and now I had a place in the sun and an inflatable yacht to play in. Katia and Stewart saw to my every need, and I didn't have to share my wealth and privilege with any other beast. This was as fabulous a life as any dog could imagine.

Despite the wall-to-wall sunshine, there were dark clouds on the horizon. Not real ones, because it was still sunny on the horizon. I'm talking about the clouds in my life, using the type of clever imagery that I don't really understand. It was all connected to that damn sailing holiday that my pet humans had taken in Greece back in the summer. They still talked about it, and in particular they still talked about that mutt they met. It was almost as if it were possible that they had space in their life for another dog besides me, which I knew was a ridiculous concept.

'Mary's still alive,' Katia said, looking at her phone as we drove back to England. 'Our sailing instructor took another group to Orei and they spotted her there. He says they gave her a meal before they left. He just e-mailed to let us know.'

So what? I asked myself. Who cares?

'Have you told him what we're thinking of doing for Mary?' asked Stewart.

'Yes,' she replied. 'He thinks it's a great idea.'

Hmph. I didn't know what all of this meant, but I took comfort from the fact that the vagrant mongrel was half a world away and would hopefully remain there.

Mary

I had been feeling odd for a while. Since the nice humans on the yacht disappeared from my life, I wasn't my usual self. My appetite grew, and that made it even harder to suppress the pain of starvation because, of course, there was no accompanying growth in my supply of food. There was only one day when I was fortunate enough to eat a full meal. The yacht returned, just for half a day, and most of the humans on board were different to the original group, but they recognised me and knew my name and made sure I was well fed before they departed.

I enjoyed that brief company of sympathetic humans, but in the following days I became listless. Something inside me wasn't normal. I grew thinner and yet I felt heavier and wearier. I left my old home beneath the wheelie bin and found somewhere more secluded next to a ridge of bushes between the beach and the park. I spent days at a time lying in the long grasses there, hiding from the other street dogs. I didn't know what was wrong with me, but if I was dying I wanted to remain in this place of quiet solitude for my final hours.

I looked down and saw that I was swollen in my middle. Pain shot through my abdomen. I grew weaker.

My life had been brief and challenging, but I was glad to have experienced it and I wouldn't have changed anything for the world. Despite all the discomfort inside me, despite all the turmoil in my distended and sickening stomach, I could still feel the sun on my fur and smell the sea in my nostrils. The pains grew more intense, but I could still appreciate the beauty of the world that I was soon to be leaving.

Pooch

About time, that's all I can say about that. In fact, I don't think I want to say anything at all now.

I'd had enough of competing for attention with this monocular Hellenic hussy. The spectre of her miserable existence hung over me all the way back to England, and for weeks after our return this wild beast seemed to be the sole topic of conversation in my house.

Every afternoon I would have a snooze and hope that the problem of my humans thinking about another dog would go away by the time I woke up. But the problem never went away, and the situation was always exacerbated by another challenge that I had to face on a daily basis: which bed to sleep in? I had a choice of several luxurious dog beds, two sofas that were apparently very expensive, and Katia's lap. I'm a lapdog. When Katia was around, I always opted for that.

On one particular afternoon, I awoke to find her in conversation with Stewart.

'When is that guy from the shelter going to collect her?' asked Stewart.

'Tomorrow, I think. He got his payment yesterday and he has a photo of Mary so he knows what she looks like.'

Shelter? What shelter? What was that all about? Were my humans hiring someone to find Mary and put her in a dog shelter? Would that involve some of that weird money stuff that could have been better spent on more toys for me to ignore?

I jumped off her lap in disgust and paced around the living room in distress. My dream life was beginning to fall apart. I couldn't escape the obvious fact that my pet humans had feelings for another dog. I had been betrayed. But it would be unhealthy for me to stew in my anger; I needed to confront them about their infidelity. I marched up to Katia, ready to resolve this ghastly situation.

Unfortunately, my attempt at reprimanding her wrongdoing was misinterpreted as a request for a biscuit. She placed a small and rather yummy treat in my mouth and I ran off with it, wagging my stump of a tail with delight. I had lost that battle, but I was determined to win the war.

Mary

I felt much better when the puppies appeared. One by one they crawled towards my belly, eyes closed, toothless and helpless. I was still technically a puppy myself, as I was less than a year old, but instinctively I knew what I had to do. I licked them and fed them. I kept them close to my body so they would be warm and safe. And I loved them. They were my precious babies. They were the only thing in my world. I had nothing else. It was too soon to worry about how I was going to find enough food to bring them all up: right now, I was the happiest dog on the planet with a family of warm hearts beating gently against my skin.

The puppies slept most of the time, soon exhausting themselves after each feed. I was unable to go anywhere while they were so vulnerable, so I closed my eye but couldn't really rest. Nowhere was truly safe for my little family and I had to remain alert. There was a potential threat from other dogs, birds of prey, rats, polecats, foxes and, sadly, humans. And it was the latter variety of danger that I had to deal with the morning after giving birth.

It was a male, and he walked alone across the beach. He saw me and turned in my direction. This automatically triggered a state of concern in me. I sat upright. I was in no mood for random affection with strangers today. The lives of my babies were at stake. I would do whatever was necessary to protect them.

Still he came closer. I put the puppies behind me and stood tall. Soon he was close enough for me to smell his odour. There was a faint suggestion of other dogs on his clothing. In one hand, he held a lead with a lasso loop. I felt the sides of my mouth retreat and the cool morning air upon my bared teeth. The man saw my snarl and stopped. He pulled a phone from his pocket and looked at something on the screen. Then he looked at me and seemed pleased, as if he recognised me. One of the puppies wriggled into view. The stranger's expression changed in an instant to one of horror. He leaned sideways and spotted the other pups. The growl came out of my mouth without me being aware of it. I would sacrifice myself to save those babies if I had to. This could be the most important moment of my life. I tensed, ready to launch myself in a full attack upon the man if he came any closer.

He stayed where he was and made a phone call.

Pooch

Just as I got myself comfortable on Katia's lap, once again, the phone rang. Katia picked me up and plonked me into a dog bed. The cheek of it! She was ignoring me completely. Her face took on an expression of surprise. She hung up and called Stewart to join her.

'It's the driver in Greece,' she told him. 'He's found Mary.'

'That's great!' said Stewart, for reasons I failed entirely to deduce.

'But it's not all good news,' she continued.

'Why? Is she hurt?'

'No, Mary's fine, but he asked me what I want to do with the puppies.'

'Puppies?' asked Stewart.

Puppies? I asked myself. This was becoming an alarming conversation.

'He said Mary has had four puppies and he wanted to know if he should bring them to the shelter as well or leave them on the beach.'

'Of course he should take them,' replied Stewart, again for reasons that escaped me.

'That's what I said,' Katia told him. 'I'll call the shelter and let them know that we'll pay for all the inoculations and food and anything else they need. And when they've all got their pet passports we'll get someone to drive all five dogs to England.'

Five dogs? That sounded like more than one. Possibly quite a lot more than one. I didn't like the sound of this at all.

Mary

He put his phone back in his pocket and backed away. I had won this fight without any injuries. My puppies were safe and I felt the tension fall away within me. I watched him intently as he retraced his steps across the beach towards the road, but he was only gone for a couple of minutes, and soon returned carrying a plastic crate. Once more I gathered the youngsters behind me and assumed my protective stance, fully prepared to lay down my life if required.

The stranger stopped and crouched low. He tried to smile, but I could tell I was making him uncomfortable. Then he reached into his pocket and produced some slices of cold meat. He threw them to me. My guard was lowered immediately. I waggled my tail and munched the food, gratefully. It was my first meal in days. I couldn't resist. Seeing that he had gained my trust, the man reached into his pocket again and produced a chunk of cheese. This time he held it in his hand for me, and I took it from him, delicately. He patted my head. By now I was practically in love with him. He gave me some more cheese. I moved aside and let him see the puppies. He held his hand for them to sniff, then he sat with me.

'Mary?' he said.

I waggled my tail. It was wonderful to hear my name again. He put his arm around me and gave me a hug. Next, he found a biscuit for me and opened the door of a crate while I was focused on eating. As he fed more biscuits to me, he slowly scooped up each of my puppies and placed them inside the crate. Then he put the lead around my neck. We were going somewhere. All of us, together. I was thrilled and nervous in equal measure.

Walking on a lead was a strange experience. I had seen other dogs on leads, and I had always envied the security and affection that a simple rope seemed to represent. A lead meant that you belonged to someone. It meant you had a home and someone to love. Dogs on leads were the uber-rich, the privileged few, and we street dogs viewed them through envious eyes. And now I was on a lead. I had a name, and a lead. I didn't think my status could ever be higher than it was at this moment. I hoped the other strays would see me proudly walking with this man. I had truly made it.

We walked along the beach towards the road and stopped at a car. I pulled back as he opened the doors. I had never been this close to a car before. Cars were to be avoided. I had seen many of my friends killed by cars – they were dangerous things –

but when he put the puppies inside I had no choice. I needed to be strong and stay with my babies. I gathered my courage and jumped in.

The smells within the car were fascinating. A blend of human and dog, plus cigarette smoke, traces of bread and other foods, and the aroma of the seat fabric and carpets. My nose was on overdrive. Then the car started to move, and I felt a sickening sensation in my stomach that I had never felt before. The car twisted and lurched, sideways, forwards, backwards. It felt as if I was being thrown around, and the uncomfortable movements continued for hours. I glanced at the puppies in their crate next to me: they were sleeping peacefully. I never got used to the motion of that car, but at least I managed to keep that precious food inside me. It would have been tragic to lose those vital calories to a dose of sickness.

I looked out of the window. I had no conception of where we were, but there was nothing familiar about the sights or the smells. Orei must have been a long way behind us. The driver turned the car into a small, rough road that led up a steep hill. The car shook noisily on the stones, waking the puppies. They crawled around inside their crate seeking the comfort of my skin and finding nothing. They needed me and I was helpless. I began to wonder if I had made a terrible mistake in submitting so readily to the temptation of food. I was starving and needed to be able to make milk for the puppies, but what good would milk do if I couldn't get to them through the bars?

Pooch

Boo hoo. Big deal. I had problems of my own, as it happens. We were talking about spending Christmas in my holiday home in Spain, and that meant I was faced with making tough choices about which toys to bring with me. There was Monster and Doobie and Roger Rabbit and Wack-Wack. They would come, no question, but there were dozens of other toys who could potentially accompany them, and there wouldn't be room for all of them. Frankly I was rather insulted that I had to leave some behind. We were going to drive to Spain in Stewart's car, but I knew that Katia had a car, too. Why couldn't we take both cars, and fill one of them with my toys? Was that so unreasonable? Of course not, but sometimes humans just don't seem to care about animals.

Katia made endless phone calls before we left. She kept calling a dog shelter in Greece to ask how Mary was doing. She negotiated with a charity that specialised in bringing dogs to England from Greece, and arranged to pay for Mary and the puppies to be included on their first run in the New Year. She received photos and video clips from the shelter, allegedly showing Mary playing with her puppies in the safety of the compound. It looked like a prison yard, and the dogs looked like filthy criminals to me.

'It's all set up,' she told Stewart as we departed for our long drive south. 'It's been a nightmare to organise, but we've done our best. The shelter can't guarantee that the puppies will survive because they're so young, but they're keeping them separate from the other dogs and the staff are disinfecting their shoes every time they go in to feed them, so that should reduce the risk of them catching something nasty.'

'And when will the van arrive to collect them all?' asked Stewart.

'In the first week of January,' she replied. 'We'll get back from Spain a day or two before they get to England, so we'll have time to prepare.'

'I'm so glad you managed to get someone to drive them for us. I'd hate to make that journey myself. Could you imagine driving that far with all those stray dogs? What a nightmare!'

I heartily agreed. I couldn't think of anything worse than a long journey in a car with a pack of wild animals with no social graces or manners. I imagined what it might be like to have them sitting beside me. I could picture them full of arrogance and attitude and ingratitude. The hellish image quickly faded from my mind as I struggled to get perfectly comfortable on the sumptuous leather seat of the Lexus, wishing the seat could be a tiny bit softer and getting annoyed that Katia didn't want me on her lap for the entire ride to Spain.

Mary

The wind blew hard at the dog shelter. We were high up a mountain near Athens, exposed to the full force of the icy *meltemi* that periodically blasted us from the north. This wasn't the kind of place I expected a dog shelter to be, though. My neighbours in the adjacent cells were not strays. They had collars and names and, most importantly, they had families.

It was in this cold cell at the dog shelter that I spent my first Christmas, and what a joyous day that was!

These dogs were just here for their holidays, and every few days a family would return to collect their dog, or another family would drop their dog off with promises of coming back soon. None of the dogs seemed to want to spend a vacation here, even though they all benefited from the safety of a concrete cell with a metal grille for a door, and had access to a concrete yard for a few hours every day. I thought they were very fortunate. And besides, they were fed in the morning *and* in the evening. Not just once a week, like I used to think would be heavenly, but twice a day! It was luxurious decadence beyond my imaginings. The man who brought me and the puppies here went away and never returned, so I still didn't consider myself to have a family, but despite that I received the same regular meals as the wealthy dogs who vacationed here, and enjoyed the same privileges of using the concrete yard for an hour or so in the morning and again in the afternoon.

My babies were growing fast. They were getting big enough to run and play and jump and chew. They were a source of joy, but also a source of exhaustion. They had endless energy and always wanted me to play with them. They now ate normal food from bowls and seemed healthy and happy, but they were quite a handful for me to control. Three boys and one girl. The people who looked after us at the shelter called the girl Sara. She had funny little ears, a dark brown head, and somewhere beneath the layers of filth on her fur there were white markings. The boys were called Shadow, Alfie and Foam. Not my choice of names, I should emphasise, but I was grateful that they had names at all. Shadow presumably got his name from the panda-like dark patches around his eyes. Alfie was smaller, more like a Jack Russell than a pure-bred mongrel like the rest of us. And Foam was the furriest: he was coated in a thick blanket of hair that made him look like a stuffed toy. They were all equally vivacious, and all utterly unlike each other in looks. It was possible that each may have had a different father, but there was no doubt in their minds that I was the mother. And yet their lives had begun so differently from mine. They had never known hunger or fear. I had managed to provide just enough milk to keep them alive whilst we were in Orei, and once we were in the shelter I was well fed and able to provide milk with ease. After they were weaned onto solid food they had never missed a meal. They were very fortunate puppies and I was pleased that they would never have to know the hardships that I had faced before they were born.

When the December winds became particularly chilling, we would huddle against each other for warmth on the concrete floor of our cell. Whoever was on the outside of the huddle would start to freeze rather quickly, so out of fairness we took turns in that position. We were never truly warm, but we were a happy family and that gave us all an inner warmth that no *meltemi* could steal.

It was in this cold cell at the dog shelter that I spent my first Christmas, and what a joyous day that was! Each of the puppies received a wonderful gift – a doggy chew. They were beside themselves with excitement and slept contentedly after an hour of intense and flavoursome chewing. And what did I get? I was given half a tennis ball. It already came with some useful bite holes, and I had the most wonderful afternoon throwing it around the concrete yard and chasing after it. I was the luckiest dog on the planet and hoped that next Christmas would be as good as this.

Pooch

My Christmas in Spain was a disaster. I can hardly bring myself to describe how awful my day was. Recounting the horrendous memories of that day makes me quiver. Where shall I begin? Firstly, I was denied a place on Katia and Stewart's bed, allegedly because I snore too much. How ridiculous! If that were really a problem, they should leave *me* on their bed while *they* come downstairs and sleep on the sofas. But my cruel humans left me instead in the living room to sleep in my fur-lined, soft doggy bed with a pretty bone motif in its lining, next to the cosy radiator. So I naturally woke up in a bad mood, and things went downhill immediately.

The first problem on that Christmas morning was the lack of sunshine. I fancied doing a bit of sunbathing next to the canal, but there were a couple of clouds lazily skimming across the sky, so I was forced to wait almost half an hour before I could feel the morning sun on my body.

The next thing to spoil my day was the topic of conversation when the humans came downstairs for breakfast. My grandparents had come to stay for Christmas, and they were talking about adopting a dog for themselves. I was insulted to think that my occasional visits to them did not constitute adequate canine companionship, but this was a difficult concept for me to deliver to them by means of a dog vocabulary consisting of a single word (you may have noticed that I seem to be somewhat more eloquent when I'm writing than when I'm barking).

The final straw was the failure of Santa Claus to fulfil my wishes. I wanted to receive an extensive list of presents on Christmas day, totalling about twenty-five items. All I got was a squeaky plastic bone, a furry bear, a furry chicken, a box of biscuits, a toy rope, a giant leather chew, a smaller leather chew, a hand-knitted winter jumper, a toy mouse, a bouncy ball, another bouncy ball that also squeaked, a cooked breakfast, a roast lunch, walkies along the beach and a cuddle from everyone in the house. Disgraceful. Barely half of what I had asked for. Everyone seemed oblivious to the cruelty I was forced to endure.

My breaking point came in the afternoon. One of our neighbours had a dog. It was a huge monster, and its mouth dribbled in a most unrefined manner. Today it decided to walk up to the fence and try to make friends with me. Such impertinence! I immediately turned my back, marched indoors, and peed on the doormat. I refuse to associate with such saliva-ridden, uncouth, unhygienic riff-raff.

Still, at least things couldn't get any worse. Or so I thought. The phone rang that evening. Katia answered it, had a brief conversation, then spoke some words I didn't want to hear (in truth, I don't want to hear most words if they're not about me).

'That was the woman from the dog transportation charity. Their driver is sick. Really sick. He's cancelled his trip to Greece.'

'Cancelled or postponed?' asked Stewart.

'Cancelled. He won't go until the spring.'

'By then the puppies will be grown and it won't be so easy to find homes for them.'

'I know. And it's really cold at the shelter during January and February. We should go and get them ourselves.'

'Drive to Greece? Are you crazy?' enquired Stewart, even though the answer to the latter question was plainly in the affirmative.

'We can't let the dogs suffer in the cold all winter,' Katia explained. 'Let's look at the map and see how to get there.'

'Cliff Richard managed it,' said Stewart, 'so I suppose it can be done, but I really don't want to drive back with all those dogs in our nice car.'

I couldn't have put it better myself. Stray dogs like Mary and her demon spawn don't belong in cars. Well, not in a Lexus, anyway. They belong in the back of a windowless, unheated van, not a luxury SUV designed for pedigrees like me.

My grandparents flew home at the beginning of January, leaving just me and Katia and Stewart. The discussion about how and whether or not to drive to Greece continued incessantly. Stewart reluctantly spent time researching ferries from Spain and from Italy, calculating mileages and routes, checking and re-checking the slowly-evolving itinerary. Eventually he committed to booking hotels and ferry crossings. I knew then that he and the voice of reason had lost the argument. We were going to drive to Greece. My perfect life was about to be ruined.

Bags appeared in the living room. Shutters were closed. Power was switched off. I was scooped up into a bag and carried to the car. This was it. The insane journey had begun. I dreaded going through with this lengthy mission. Within moments I had forgotten where we were going and why. I fell asleep and dreamed I was tall enough to look down on a kitten.

Cannes was everything I dreamed it would be. A motel surrounded by grass that smelled of the excrement of exotic Poodles and other pleasant stinks. I spent a comfortable night there, wedged between my pet humans, taking up the majority of the double bed despite my diminutive body. I woke them well before dawn, just to be certain that they would not get enough sleep, and demanded to return to the grass outside so that I could contribute my own special smell to the general ambience.

No-one mentioned Mary that morning. No one talked about Greece. The spectre of the stray dog began to retreat. I relaxed. Later that morning I took my humans across the border into Italy and we stopped at a colourful harbour town called Portofino. The car park was full of Ferraris and Bentleys and other wonderful vehicles that would have been suitable for a dog like me. We dined on the quayside, enjoying the warm January sunshine and watching the boats. Apparently, Mary lived in a place like this. As I nibbled the pieces of grilled chicken and matured cheeses that were handed to me under the table, and then washed it down with half a cup of mineral water, I couldn't see what the fuss was all about. Living on the quayside of a harbour didn't seem so bad.

The dogs in Portofino were very refined. They wore diamond-encrusted collars, they walked proud and upright, and their pee smelled like a fine white wine. Perhaps I had been wrong about Mary. If she was living like these Italian dogs, she must be almost as classy as me. But it didn't seem to matter now.

Mary was not the topic of conversation today. We were heading to our next objective, a town called Pisa. It seemed I had underestimated my humans. This wasn't a rescue mission to Greece. This was a cultural tour of Italy, all for my benefit.

We arrived at Pisa in late afternoon. The sun was beginning to set, and I was desperate to spend a penny. Unfortunately, I had no option but to pee against an old tower, and it was leaning so much that the pee kept flowing back towards my feet. I wasn't impressed with Pisa. If they couldn't be bothered to build their towers straight for the convenience of Yorkshire Terriers needing to relieve themselves, then I had no respect for Italian culture. I decided not to stay in any town that had yet to discover the spirit level. I took my humans back to the car and headed in search of a hotel.

We stopped at the resort of San Vincenzo. It was late evening, and there wasn't time to find a dog-friendly hotel, so we settled on Hotel Il Delfino. This means 'Hotel The Dolphin'. Apparently soggy sea mammals are more welcome than their furry cousins. Katia placed me inside a bag and told me to keep quiet. She held me behind her while we checked in at the front desk, and she only let me out once we were safely in our room. A double bed and a single bed. What luxury. I immediately chose the double bed for myself. Katia would have to share the single with Stewart. For some reason this plan did not work out, however, and I was forced to endure the humiliation of sleeping alone in a single bed.

My presence in the hotel remained a secret from the staff. And by staff, I mean the old woman who owned it and her husband who sat in the lounge reading a newspaper. This was January, of course; not even the dolphins came on holiday at this time of year. In the morning, I peed on the balcony, returned to my executive transportation bag, and Katia carried me to the car where I waited while the humans had their breakfast. I had managed to stay in a glamorous three-star hotel without paying. That felt good.

There followed a gloriously sunny drive along the coastal road from San Vincenzo down towards Rome, passing an almost unknown island called Giglio. Just three days later, an ill-fated cruise ship, the *Costa Concordia*, would cause that island to lose its anonymity for ever. We pressed on past Rome, by-passed the crowded streets of Naples, and arrived in the shadow of a rather ominous-looking volcano.

Mount Vesuvius.

Tonight's hotel was somewhat more civilised than the previous one. Dogs were welcome, and I was given the option of walking from the car to the room.

However, I still chose to be carried, since this was a more appropriate way for me to arrive. Stewart was desperate for a genuine Italian pizza that night, but despite walking for an hour and finding several restaurants, we couldn't find a single pizzeria. So it was back to the hotel for a simple supper of steak with blue cheese sauce and gratin potatoes. I don't recall what Katia and Stewart had.

My cultural tour of Italy continued the next morning with a visit to the ruins of Pompeii.

The ruins of Pompeii are now a World Heritage Site, which made it especially satisfying as I went around peeing on them.

This had apparently been a thriving town two thousand years ago, but an eruption of the volcano tragically cost the lives of hundreds of dogs. Oh, and about twenty thousand humans. The entire fabric of the town was still there, streets and houses and shops, all looking quite normal except for the absence of roofs. The ruins are now a World Heritage Site, which made it especially satisfying as I went around peeing on them.

And talking of dogs, the place was infested with lazy Italian strays. And I mean, really lazy. They did nothing but sleep and lollop around, refusing to work, living off hand-outs and always expecting something for nothing. I was disgusted at their workshy culture of entitlement, and tried hard to remove them from my mind as I scratched at Katia's leg and demanded a biscuit and a cuddle.

After a few hours in Pompeii I decided that I had marked enough territory for the whole town to be mine. We could leave, safe in the knowledge that my property empire had expanded. To be honest I wasn't sure I really wanted a city in ruins as part of my portfolio, but the proximity to a volcano meant that it was probably a nice, warm place to be.

We checked out of the hotel before the next eruption and spent the afternoon driving across Italy towards its eastern coast, arriving at the port town of

Bari. Ominously we made no attempt to find a hotel. Something was not right. Katia had passports in her hand. Stewart drove us to a line of cars next to a ship. We were about to board a ferry, but where to? I had no idea where you could visit by ferry from Italy. Australia? The North Pole? Mars? Katia carried me to our cabin and fed me. Today had been exhausting. I didn't wake up until we were sailing into the Greek port of Patras.

I yawned and stretched. I'd heard of Greece. Couldn't quite place it in my little brain this morning, though. Something to do with John Travolta? The condition of my silky coat? The word 'Greece' didn't connect with anything. I peed on the deck of the ferry before returning to the car and driving onto land.

We didn't remain in Patras long. In a few minutes, we were on a motorway and whizzing eastwards towards Athens. I still didn't make the connection. At the back of my mind was a general sense of unease about being here, but since there's very little room at the back of my mind – or in any other part of it, for that matter – I couldn't focus those concerns into anything that made sense. Athens came and went. We sped past it on the motorway and continued to Keratea and then turned right towards nowhere in particular. At nowhere we turned left onto a dirt track and started to drive uphill. The road twisted its way up the mountainside, another volcano perhaps? But this place was nothing like Pompeii. I just couldn't figure out where we were and why we were here.

My blissful ignorance ended the second I heard a dog barking. Its voice was joined by others, and soon an entire canine choir was echoing around the hills. This was the prison where Mary was being held. I just knew it.

Mary

The kind lady at the shelter who had been looking after me and my puppies came to see me. She told me I had visitors, but why anyone would ask to visit me was a mystery. I had never received a visitor in my life. I became extremely excited as she opened the door to let me and the babies into the little courtyard where we exercised every morning. We jumped over each other and wrestled and chased, and completely forgot that someone was coming. In the chaos of four hyper-active puppies all demanding that I play with them, I didn't notice when two people walked into the enclosure. I heard the name 'Mary' mentioned, but there wasn't time to look up at my visitors. Their smell stirred vague memories which were instantly buried by the mass of swirling puppies around my head. I got the impression they were trying to take photos of us and of my shy neighbour, a huge and fluffy Siberian Husky called Hermes, but after a few minutes the visitors had gone and we were all back in our luxurious concrete and steel cell.

Pooch

I didn't understand it – which is not unusual, given that I'm marginally less intelligent than a flea. Katia and Stewart seemed to have driven for many days to get to this horrible dog prison in Greece, then visited it for five or ten minutes, and now we were driving away again. I had waited in the car the whole time, and had not been required to sully myself by mixing with the canine riff-raff that frequented that institution, and when we left I was still the only dog in the family. It was a relief, of course, but it didn't make sense. My humans smuggled me into a hotel that night, and, as usual, I slept in the centre of the bed taking up nearly all the space.

I didn't know it then, but that was to be the last night that I would ever have my pet humans to myself.

I was given strict instructions to keep quiet in the morning. The chain-smoking owner of the little hotel had no sympathy for dogs, apparently, and it was essential that I made no sounds while Katia carried me through the lobby. Through the gap in my personal carry bag I spied the owner sitting behind his desk, obscured in a cloud of smoke, grumbling in a strange language. Stewart gave him some money while Katia continued towards the door. But something was tickling my throat. A wisp of smoke had filtered into my bag. I couldn't hold back any longer and released a bout of coughing that made the bag shake and caused the Greek man to stand up and look at Katia suspiciously. After the coughing had finished I tried to clear my throat, which sounded as if I was throwing up. It was only because the Greek man's utter inability to speak English was matched by Stewart and Katia's total lack of Greek that we were able to avoid being shouted at and fined for breaking the rules of this rather grim establishment. I felt the bag swing vigorously as Katia swept me out of the lobby and into the car. A close escape, but we had got away with it. Now our holiday in Greece was over and we could go home, where I would continue to rule my little kingdom, unchallenged.

But we didn't go straight home. We went back to that dog prison on the mountain, back to those criminal, low-class mutts who were unworthy to sniff my backside. Again, I waited. Katia went to see those horrendous hounds while Stewart began to do strange things to the car. He squashed all of our luggage into the space on the floor between the front and back seats, and placed a pile of bags in the centre of the back seat, leaving a space for two people with no legs (for there was no place for the feet) in the back seats. He placed wee-wee pads everywhere, and put one of my toys on each of the two spaces he'd left in the back. Then he disappeared for a moment and returned with a large dog crate. He washed it with a hosepipe, dried it with paper towels, and then placed it in the rear of the car. It was far too big for me, and I was too important to travel in the boot, anyway. So it was a pointless thing for him to do. Another strange thing that he did was take a couple of old sweatshirts from one of the bags and put them on the backs of the two front seats, with the hoodies covering the headrests. These seats had internal heating, installed for my benefit. They didn't need to wear clothes as well.

While I pondered on all these weird occurrences, Stewart left me alone and went to join Katia. Moments later he returned with one of the inmates from this prison. From my position on the front seat I strained to see the vile creature. It was hard to see the monster's face, but I could tell it was an uneducated beast, unfamiliar with the etiquette of walking on a lead and completely untamed.

'Don't worry, Mary,' I heard Stewart say. 'It's OK. You're going to live with us, now.'

My little heart sank. I was about to meet my nemesis. Stewart opened the back door and tried to persuade the stray to jump in. She didn't have a clue what he meant. Reluctantly he crouched down and picked her up, delivering her to the space he had made in one half of the back seat. He closed the door and looked at himself in disgust. That dog was filthy, and now he was, too. Served him right for touching any dog besides me. I'm always clean, thanks to my annual bath.

I could smell Mary in the seat behind me. It wasn't pretty. I looked at her, and counted the eyes. One. Well, that doesn't mean much because I can usually only count to one anyway, so any dog I look at will have a total of one eye, but I also counted the missing eyes and that also came to one, so this was definitely the Mary I had been forced to hear so much about. There was a huge, silly smile on her face. She had no appreciation for the fact that she was sitting in the back of a Lexus, where she patently did not belong. She was just gormlessly, deliriously happy for no apparent reason. She was in my car, and in my life. It had finally happened.

I sighed. This was the day my life of thoroughly-deserved privilege would end.

Mary

I was in a car. I grinned. This was the day my life would really begin. In the front of the car was a small dog. He was adorable. He was my new brother. I smiled at him and sniffed him. He smelled odd. It was a smell I had not encountered before on a dog. It took me a while to place it. He was clean. A clean dog. Well, there was a first time for everything. I decided I loved my brother already and we would become best friends.

I was soon joined on the back seat by another dog. I knew this dog. He was Hermes, my shy Husky neighbour in the shelter. I smiled at him and he looked at the floor. Soon the sounds of chaos approached. My puppies. They were spinning and jumping and running and demonstrating clearly that they had never been walked on leads before. One by one they were scooped up and placed into a crate behind me in the car. I found their smells reassuring. If this was my new family, it was huge and it was wonderful.

A man and a woman climbed into the front seats and we drove off. Wondrous sights flashed by me – trees, houses, horses, and cars. I caught hints of their aromas through the car's ventilation system. I was so consumed with anticipation and excitement that I didn't notice when we stopped after just a few minutes.

We had arrived at a veterinary surgery. So the legends were true. There really were people who took care of sick animals. How lovely! A kind vet lady inspected each of us, gave us little treats, and wrote things down in blue booklets. These booklets were passports, and one of them was mine. I had a passport. Not only did I have a name, I had official documentation. My head swelled so much with pride that I wondered if I would fit through the door. Everyone had a quick pee-pee outside the clinic – well, everyone apart from the humans for some reason – and then we climbed back into the car and continued our journey.

The car seat was soft in a way that I had never felt before. It was like sitting on a pile of puppies. I had never dreamed that such luxury existed. I soon felt sleepy amid this sumptuous comfort and closed my eye.

Pooch

For a few minutes after the visit to the vet I clung to the fantasy that the stinky dogs in the back of my car would be returned to their prison. Or that their sentences were complete and they could be released back onto the streets of Greece. My dreams did not come true. The creatures continued their illegal squatting in my Lexus. They didn't speak much, but when they did I had no idea what they were saying. It was all Greek to me.

At a motorway toll booth Katia opened her window. The woman inside the booth recoiled at the stench that flowed from inside my car. I felt embarrassed, and tried to explain that it wasn't me, but my explanation was misinterpreted as a yawn. The woman maintained a look of serene pity while her face turned blue from holding her breath whilst taking our money. I put my super-sensitive nose to use and tried to analyse the aromas emanating from behind me. There was a new whiff. I knew the puppies' fur was encrusted with things unmentionable, but something else was competing for dominance in my vast nasal spectrum. Something that had come from the opposite end. The puppies were throwing up inside their cramped cage in the boot area.

This revelation gave me hope. I never vomit in cars. Stewart and Katia were not used to this kind of infringement of their clean air. Perhaps it would convince them of the error of their ways and trigger a return to the prison camp for those dogs? I waited for the car to turn around and head back to where we had started our journey, but no such U-turn occurred. Instead, we pulled over at the next motorway services and while Katia attempted to walk all four insane puppies at the same time, Stewart washed the unpleasantness from their cage. With the puppies relieved and returned to their incarceration, Mary and Hermes the Husky took the opportunity to jump out and mark some territory. And when that was done, finally, it was my turn. I was the last dog out of seven to be allowed out of the car for a pee. The last. Think about it. Why would they leave me until last? It could only mean one thing: I was the most important animal in the car, and they wanted to save the best until last. It was the only explanation that made sense. I contentedly peed on Stewart's shoe and returned to the car with my head held high, waiting to be picked up and put back inside.

Stewart drove us to the port at Patras at a relaxed pace, calculating that he would arrive two hours before the ferry to Italy was due to depart and not wishing to spend too long queuing for the ship. But he's not smart like me: he had made a miscalculation that could have condemned us to an extra day in the car with nowhere to go. As Katia handed over the ferry ticket at the gate the man looked at his watch and spoke to her,

'The ship sails in fifteen minutes. If you go quickly you might just make it.'

But we had seven dogs on board. It wasn't an option just to drive straight on. We had to go to the office and show our passports and collect the boarding passes. Stewart screeched the car to a halt outside the ferry company's office and sprinted inside. Meanwhile Katia frantically tried to get us all to pee, which was challenging given the absence of grass and lampposts. Flustered and stressed, Stewart returned ten minutes later and drove at full speed towards the ship. We were the last car up the ramp. It closed behind us. We weren't even inside the vessel – the only remaining parking space was where the car deck was open to the sky.

'Why is the ship sailing two hours early?' asked Katia.

'The ticket uses the twenty-four hour clock,' he replied. 'I read seventeen hundred hours as seven o'clock, not five.'

Idiot, I thought to myself, wondering why we were all swaying slightly.

Mary

The excitement continued. What a day! The long, pungent ride in the car with my puppies, my nervous neighbour and my fabulous new brother, the pee-pee stops, the scent of vomit and now the aroma of an oily car deck, my senses were bursting with wonder. We walked from the car into a small room. Electronic sliding doors closed us in. When they opened a few moments later we were somewhere else, transported magically from the car deck to the top of the ship. The salty sea air blew gently through my fur coat. I grinned at my babies in their crate. They wriggled and played as one of my new humans painfully dragged their bulky container along the deck to the ship's kennels.

Here we were shown our accommodation for the voyage. It seemed I had hit the jackpot yet again. The puppies shared a kennel together, but Hermes and I each had a private cell to ourselves. And what a cell! I had my own steel door and my own concrete floor which sloped down towards a gutter. When the humans had finished putting us in our cages they then provided us with bowls of water and a blanket to lie on. We were such lucky dogs.

Pooch

I laughed as I watched the filthy dogs incarcerated in a lowly manner, befitting of their status. I knew the cell block wasn't to be my destination, and I was right. With the strays all locked up, I was led downstairs to a proper cabin for humans. Well, strictly speaking it was a 'dog-friendly' cabin, which meant the floor was washable for some reason.

'Lucky those kennels were available,' said Katia. 'I don't think our original plan of sharing this cabin with all seven of them would have worked.'

'I had no idea the dogs would be so dirty,' said Stewart, clearly not including me in his comment. 'I don't think we can stay in that dog-friendly hotel I booked for us in Switzerland.'

'Shall we just cancel the hotel and drive through the night without stopping?'

'We have no choice,' he replied.

'But you're rubbish at staying awake. You're always asleep by eleven.'

'I know. But we're on this boat for almost twenty-four hours. I should sleep as much as possible in preparation.'

That, I decided, was a good plan for me, too. Imagine my horror and chagrin, therefore, when my snoring was disturbed in order for me to do some kind of work.

Work? I didn't know the meaning of the word. Nor did I want to. Work was not for lapdogs. Work was not for superior hounds like me. Work was something *other* dogs did, and I had no desire to understand what that even meant, but Katia had somehow got it into her head that I could be useful in some capacity. As she carried me up the stairs to the top deck of the ship, I thought about it. I was not designed to be useful. I served no purpose, and nor should I. I was created to sponge off society. I was destined for a life of free food, shelter and affection and I should not have to give anything in return except the unquestionable pleasure of my company. I was useless and proud of it. And yet, here I was on a ship being told that I had some service to perform. What could it possibly be?

We arrived at the block of kennels. The Greek beasts began to bark. I waggled my tail to hide my disapproval of their foreign tongue. Katia placed me on a bench and told me to wait there. Of course, I was too lazy to disobey. She disappeared amongst the kennels, then returned with four feral puppies.

'Come on Pooch,' she said, picking me up again and plonking me gracelessly on the cold, steel deck.

'I need you to teach the puppies how to walk on a lead.'

Me? Teach? That was a serious job with responsibilities. What was my pay? What were the holiday entitlements? What were the hours? Before I could discuss any such contractual matters I found myself clipped to a lead and being led up and down the deck, followed just inches behind by the rowdy rabble of puppies. I didn't want them sniffing me, so I marched briskly along, trying always to keep them behind me. And apparently that's what I was supposed to do. I guess I'm just a natural at teaching. By walking in a straight line on a lead I was inadvertently showing the guttersnipes how to do it. Within minutes their wild gyrations at the end of their tethers settled down into a more measured gait. They got used to the leads and they followed my example of how walkies works. I have to admit I felt rather chuffed at my success as an educator. The puppies were now less annoying and I felt a weird sensation inside me. I wasn't sure what it was, because it wasn't something I'd come across before, but I think it had something to do with a sense of achievement, a sense of satisfaction at having done something good for the world. I decided I quite liked that feeling, although I would have preferred to have

achieved it without having had to get up from my
bed.

Mary

I was so proud of my babies. Katia – for I had now deduced that she, like me, had a name – spent hours on the doggy deck with them, teaching them to walk, to sit, to pay attention and to be good. OK, perhaps not exactly good, but a goal of making them slightly less naughty than normal seemed to be not too unrealistic. At one point, when we were all on the deck together, the captain of the ship came outside and expressed his surprise that she was travelling with so many dogs. He seemed to think she was crazy, for some reason. I still didn't know where we were going, but I hoped the captain had some idea, and I trusted him to get us there, wherever that was. My little baby brother Pitz was fantastic at showing the puppies the way, encouraging them to follow him as Katia repeatedly walked them up and down.

We spent a long but comfortable night in our first-class cages, and were overjoyed to see Katia arrive with our breakfast in the morning. The delicious meal of dry food was followed by more exercise and training on the deck. It made us all feel incredibly important, as if we had been selected for special training for our new life. Clearly, the ability to walk in a more-or-less straight line was going to be essential to our future roles in society, and we all put in a huge effort to rise to the challenge of not running in circles or random directions like we were used to doing.

In the afternoon of our second day at sea we returned to the vehicle deck and took our places in the car. I'd heard that Greece had many islands. I wondered which one we were about to explore.

Pooch

We departed the ship at somewhere called Ancona and immediately joined the city's evening rush hour, and I could tell Stewart was stressed by this. He didn't enjoy driving through Italy. He refused to give me any attention and sat behind the wheel, fuming and complaining and looking at his watch. Apparently, we only had about eighteen hours to get from the Adriatic Sea to the English Channel. Sounded long enough to me. The satnav said we could do it in fourteen. I curled up on my cushion and dozed off.

I woke up to the sound of the car horn blaring. Stewart was driving angrily with one hand permanently hovering over the hooter, repeatedly attempting to alert Italian drivers to their violations of the British Highway Code as they drifted randomly from lane to lane on the motorway without signals or common sense, all whilst talking on mobile phones. They apparently had no awareness of something called lane 'discipline', whatever that was, and Stewart's stress increased as he tried to avoid being hit by drivers who laboured under the misapprehension that they had the road all to themselves. After this had been going on for some hours, he postulated a theory. Italians talk with their hands. And they needed both hands to talk. So when chatting on a phone whilst driving, they would have to wedge their mobile between their shoulder and their chin in order to free up sufficient hands to accompany their words. I'm neither a mathematician nor an anatomist (nor many other things, but they're not relevant in the context of this anecdote), but if a person uses both hands for talking and a shoulder to keep the phone to their ear, there are not many body parts remaining with which they can steer a car.

'They drive like children,' I heard him say as we dodged our way around the Milan by-pass. 'I can drive the length of Britain or France or even Greece and not use the horn once. In Italy, I have to use it every couple of minutes.'

So it was with great relief when, after six hours of Italian roads and with midnight approaching, we crossed the border into Switzerland. I could sense Stewart relaxing. We had managed to get through Italy without a scratch on the car, but now we faced a new challenge. It was January and we were at the bottom of a mountain range. Stewart expressed his new concern.

'What if there's too much snow? We might not make it across the Alps,' he said.

What were we? The Von Trapp Canine Singers? I wasn't worried. Nor was anyone else. Katia was asleep. Mary and Hermes were asleep, and even the puppies in the boot were silent. As it turned out, we didn't drive over the Alps, anyway. We drove beneath them in endless tunnels that were reassuringly free of snow. It took just over three hours to cross from one side of Switzerland to the other. We entered France at three in the morning. Stewart was exhausted. He had used up his supply of energy drinks and was struggling to stay awake. At the first motorway services we came to, he pulled into the car park and fell instantly asleep in the driving seat with the engine still running to keep us all warm.

Ten minutes later he was wide awake. Rebooted and recharged. He climbed outside and stretched his legs, peed against a tree, then returned to the car. We left the eerie, abandoned car park and re-joined the motorway where a patch of very intense and frightening fog enveloped us.

No longer able to travel at the permitted speed limit, we slowed to a crawl. Stewart seemed unhappy about this. I turned over and went back to sleep. Many more brief motorway services stops followed, each lasting just long enough for Stewart to take a power nap, and each time I was awoken by a blast of icy January night air as he opened his door to stretch. We were now in northern France, zipping from one patch of dark and freezing fog to the next, along roads that were almost deserted. Stewart was getting delirious with fatigue, and needed to pull over and stop to close his eyes just for a couple of minutes every half an hour.

The signs for the Channel Tunnel appeared soon after dawn. Stewart was at breaking point, but our destination was in sight. We turned off the motorway and threaded our way to the Pet Reception Centre to get the doggy passports checked. It was one last chance for me to be rid of the strays. All the hounds were fully immunised and medicated according to the latest British laws, but if they didn't pass this bureaucratic hurdle they wouldn't be allowed into England, and I would remain unchallenged in my role as head of the family.

Just for once it appeared that my dreams had come true. Stewart and Katia led us all into the Pet Reception Centre and handed over a pile of pet passports.

The chip in my neck was scanned by the wonderful French gentleman who worked in the Pet Reception Centre. He cross-checked the number against my passport, checked that my paperwork was satisfactory, and issued a document to allow me to travel to England. I should blooming well hope so, too. He then came to Mary, Hermes, and the puppies. All of their chips scanned perfectly, but when he inspected their passports he looked Stewart in the eye and told him there was a problem with all six documents: none of the Greek dogs could be permitted to travel to England.

I don't know if it's really possible to fall in love at first sight, but I wanted to adopt this Frenchman. He was divine. He had permitted me to enter the castle and pulled up the drawbridge before the other dogs could follow. He was my hero.

Stewart, on the other hand, did not see this development in the same positive way that I did. Perhaps it was the fact that he had been driving all night, crossing three countries on a charitable rescue mission, only to be told it was all for nothing.

With seemingly endless patience, the adorable Frenchman explained the problem. The pet passport was only valid if the animal had been seen by a vet and given a tapeworm treatment. This medication had to be dispensed not more than five days and not less than twenty-four hours before arriving in England. The pet passport contained two boxes in which the vet is supposed to write the date and the time of the treatment. Fortunately, the Greek vet had written the date in both boxes, and the time in neither. It was three days since we had been to the vet in Greece to get those treatments – right in the middle of the approved time window for entry into England. Obviously the tapeworm medicine had been given at the appropriate time, but because the specific time of day had not been recorded, the passports were invalid.

This did not go down well with Katia or Stewart. After a sleepless night, this was not the kind of obstacle they were capable of handling in a dignified manner. They started to let the man know what they thought of him. When that didn't work, they questioned the logic of his decision. When he held his position, they fumed. They ranted. They almost cried. Though to be honest, I'm not entirely sure what they did or said because I was too busy running around in circles out of pure joy. Would they release the strays in the car park now? Or would they give them to the man at the Pet Reception Centre and let him keep them? Katia seemed almost ready to do that.

'This is a charitable rescue,' she told him. 'Those dogs have been in the car for seventeen hours. It's cruel to delay us. They've had the treatment required by law and they should be allowed to travel.'

'The paperwork must be correct,' he repeated. 'We are not allowed to let any animals travel if there is a mistake in their passports.'

'But we've crossed four frontiers already to get here,' Katia screeched. 'No one said there was a problem with the documents. In fact, all of the border guards in other countries actually praised us for what we are doing.'

'It is not my fault,' he explained. 'Your vet in Greece has made a mistake with all of these passports. Where the tapeworm treatment is recorded, he has written the date but not the time. We need to have both, because the animal must enter the UK between one and five days after the treatment. You must go back to your vet.'

'The vet is in Greece!' shouted Katia. 'We can't get her to change it now.'

'If you can get her to fax a letter to us stating the time that she gave the treatments, I will accept that. Until then, you cannot travel.'

We left the building and returned to the car. Katia and Stewart loaded us all back into our respective portions of the Lexus and then searched for a phone number to call the vet in Greece. No answer. Katia phoned the kennel from where we had collected the foul beasts. The kennel owner informed Katia that the vet had told her she would be working on a remote farm today with some sheep and would be out of contact. There was no hope of resolving the situation.

I don't think I've ever been happier than at that point.

Katia couldn't face the Frenchman again. Stewart took a deep breath and returned to the building to tell him the vet could not be reached. Some other solution had to be possible. Moments later he returned with a piece of paper, and my joyful state evaporated.

'There's a vet here in Calais,' he said. 'Apparently he can fix the passports for a fee. The man in the Pet Reception Centre has phoned ahead to tell him we're coming. This is the address.'

He passed the piece of paper to Katia. She tapped the address into the satnav while Stewart started driving us to the centre of Calais. It was a treacherous journey, carried out at high speed and with clumsy control. Stewart was beyond tired. He didn't need this. We should have been on the tunnel train and getting half an hour of sleep, not making a pointless detour into a busy town. He bumped the car up onto the sidewalk and ran into the veterinary surgery, clutching the six passports.

We waited in the car. And waited. And waited. After a while we were all asleep, and woke with a jolt when Stewart yanked the door open and threw the passports onto Katia's lap.

'Let's go!' he shouted, putting the car in gear and throwing us all around as he swerved back onto the road.

'Why did it take so long?' Katia asked.

'The place was packed,' he replied. 'The vet was telling all of his French customers to be quick because he had a train to catch in fifteen minutes. Other pet owners arrived and were, inevitably, seen before me, because they were French which gives them automatic priority. And then, when I was the only one left, the vet put on his coat and started to walk out.'

'What?' she asked.

'I couldn't believe it. I shouted "*Monsieur – les passeports!*" and I held out the six pet passports. The vet shrugged and pointed at his receptionist before marching out the door. He didn't even look at them.'

'The receptionist fixed them?'

'Yes,' he replied. 'She just took the passports and filled in the boxes correctly, then signed and stamped them. For a fee, of course.'

'What a racket.'

'Precisely.'

I didn't approve, either. The dogs were legal. There was now nothing to stop them invading my home.

And just four hours later, that is exactly what those matted, encrusted, odoriferous street urchins did.

Mary

My, oh my, oh my, oh my! What wonders were these? What was this miraculous place to which we had been delivered? I couldn't understand it. How could so many beautiful things be waiting for us? We were led from the car to a gate. And it was behind this gate that the wonders appeared. I chased all of my puppies across the gravel towards something peculiar and green. I had never seen anything like it before. None of us had. It was soft and springy, wide and flat. I since learned that it's called grass and this was a lawn.

I had never seen anything like it before. It was soft and springy,
wide and flat. I since learned that it's called grass.
It felt heavenly under my paws.

It felt heavenly under my paws. I had never played on such a gentle surface before. The puppies were in ecstasy, and we ran and ran and ran in circles, in squares, in straight lines and in slaloms. I was incapable of measuring the vastness of my delight. My grin was so wide I was afraid I might swallow one of the puppies. I didn't think things could get any better, but then they did. Katia dragged out a ball from under a bush and threw it for us.

A toy! A real toy! I had only ever played with dried poo and stones when I was on the streets. Even in the shelter I only played with half a ball. This was a complete ball, and it had far superior characteristics: it bounced, and, er, well, it kept on bouncing. What more do you need? It was fabulous. Our insane running around went up a gear. Now the ball drove us all wild. It was the best day ever.

Pooch

It was the worst day ever. I sat on the steps at the back of my house and watched my lovely lawn being overrun by a rabble of Greek invaders. They tore up my lawn with their claws until it looked like a First World War battlefield. They disturbed the silence that it was my right alone to disturb. They rolled in my poo. And then, the final insult, they started playing with my tennis ball. I couldn't bear it. My universe was collapsing around me. I barked for someone to let me into the kitchen, but Katia and Stewart were too preoccupied with the new dogs to pay any attention to me. Imagine that! My orders went unheeded. This was unheard of. I scratched some paint off the back door and barked again, but still no one came.

I had been abandoned. I had lost everything. I was no better than a stray, destined to roam the streets hungry, unwanted, lonely. My stumpy tail lowered. I hung my head. How could it have come to this? What could I have done wrong? Obviously that was a rhetorical question, whatever that is, because I'm a perfect dog and I couldn't possibly have done anything wrong. The fault lay entirely with the intruders. I was blameless, but that didn't change the fact that my life was ruined.

When finally the back door opened and I walked into my house, I was trampled by a herd of beasts. They pushed and shoved and jumped over me and gave me none of the respect that I am always due. Now they were in my home and things were about to deteriorate to depths that were previously beyond my imaginings.

Mary

What on earth was this strange place into which we had stumbled? I had scarcely recovered from the immense joy of experiencing a supple lawn for the first time when I found myself in a fresh wonderland. I had barely noticed it before, but next to the garden in which we were playing was a building. It was one of those large kennels that humans live in. It had always been my dream to see inside one of them, but I never thought it would actually happen. I found myself in a kaleidoscope of smells and a bewildering array of *things*. What were all these things that humans kept in their homes? I'd spent some time in a dog kennel, and I was fortunate enough to have had a bowl, a bed, and a floor that was occasionally clean, but the human kennel was different. In front of me was a large, oblong item. It was covered in fabric and was low at the front, with a ledge and a high back. I jumped on it and found it to be the softest, springiest thing on which I had ever jumped. I walked around it in a tight circle, thinking it would make a suitable bed for a king of dogs.

'Get off, Mary!' hollered Katia. So now I knew what it was called. It was called Mary, just like me. I wondered how many other things were also called Mary. Perhaps it wasn't such a special name, after all? I jumped off the Mary, only to be replaced immediately by two of my puppies who started tumbling over each other across Mary's bounciest bits. I sensed they were being naughty, so I did what I always did in that situation and pretended they were nothing to do with me.

Back in the garden, Stewart was trying to bring things under control. And he was failing completely. I ran to him and stood attentively by his side, and watched with contented curiosity as he attempted to pluck a puppy from the whirlwind of fur and dribble and big smiles that had engulfed his property.

When I had had my fill of viewing this chaos, I returned to the human kennel and threaded a path between several large puddles of pee-pee towards another room. This room smelled of food. I decided to spend lots of time in this room. On the floor was a bowl containing some meat. I chomped it down in seconds before any other dogs had a chance to find it. My stomach thanked me as I returned to the garden to be silly.

On the floor was a bowl containing some meat.
I chomped it down in seconds.

Pooch

I went to the kitchen, head bowed, ears floppy and listless. It would be my last refuge, a place from which I could defend my food until I could be bothered to eat it. I approached my little bowl on the floor: it was empty. Licked clean. I sniffed it. There was a stench of Greek stray lingering in the air. I was furious. With no food to guard I walked over to my box of toys. I had dozens of toys – teddy bears, ropes, squeaky things, baby toys and balls. Some of these toys were more than ten years old, and they had survived because my jaws are too feeble to be able to rip them apart like bigger dogs are prone to do. By careful hoarding and playing gently during my whole life, I had enough toys for an entire street full of dogs, and they were all mine. I was determined to keep it that way.

The toy box was almost empty. I stared in horror at the scene of desecration. Most of the toys were gone. I looked around and saw pieces of stuffing on the floor. The shredded entrails of my bestest friends. I felt sick. I had never before seen the guts of my toys spread out in such a gory scene. I went outside to get some air. There I beheld the sight that no dog should have to witness: six dogs were playing with my toys, having fun. It was disgraceful. They were throwing them, chewing them, ripping them to pieces. The toys I had treasured for years had been reduced to empty sacks of fake fur, squeakies without the squeak, balls that would no longer bounce.

I stared in horror at the scene of desecration.

I ordered them to cease and desist with immediate effect, but despite using my most authoritative bark no-one paid any attention to the yapping Yorkie on the back steps. I was being robbed in broad daylight and no one was there to help. Katia and Stewart even seemed complicit in the crimes. They actively encouraged the imposter dogs to play with my toys, and seemed to find it amusing to witness the demise of my treasured possessions.

Only one small incident that day managed to raise my spirits briefly. Mary started to walk in circles and ended up squatting over Gabriela's grave where she duly deposited the remains of everything she had eaten between Greece and here. A lack of respect for a late cat was something I could admire. Perhaps Mary was not totally bad after all? Perhaps we shared a common bond of feline phobia? But then I remembered all of the negative things that accompanied Mary's presence here, and I knew I was fooling myself (which, admittedly, isn't usually very hard to do). A shared disrespect of dead moggies was never going to compensate for the emotional damage I was experiencing at this cataclysmic change to my home and my lifestyle. The last time I had been here, everything I surveyed was mine, mine, mine. I had shared nothing, and never wanted to. This was nothing short of robbery.

Mary

Back in the kitchen, I took a moment amid the joyous celebrations of our new surroundings to sniff the bottom of my new little brother, Pitz, or Pooch, as Katia and Stewart seemed to prefer to call him. What a generous soul he was. How incredibly warm-hearted of him to share his toys, his garden and his home with us. I expressed my gratitude for his magnanimity by licking his face, but he somehow must have misinterpreted my gesture because he snapped and growled at me and then ran away. Oh well, I guessed there would be plenty of opportunities to bond with him in the future.

And what a future it would be! I was bristling with delicious anticipation of the games we would play and the bones we would share.

In the next room, Stewart was moving furniture to create a blockade in one corner. He put a large doggy bed and a bowl of water into the segregated space, then began herding the puppies into it. When all four of my babies were there, everything calmed down. They relaxed in their enclosure, they slowed down, and they peed all over the floor. Hermes crawled under the coffee table and went to sleep. Pooch was having fun playing hide-and-seek all by himself. I climbed back onto the Mary and got myself comfortable.

'Sorry, Mary,' said Katia. 'The sofa is not for dogs.'

I had no idea what that meant, so I smiled at her and closed my eye. I heard her sigh, then felt the cushion move as she sat next to me.

I had never experienced such love and luxury and safety before. I was free from worries. I was happier than I'd ever thought possible.

When she stroked my head I felt shivers run down my spine and I purred like one of those cat creatures (you know the ones I mean – small and creepy and very chaseable). I had never experienced such love and luxury and safety before. I was free from worries. I was happier than I'd ever thought possible.

As I drifted into a blissful unconsciousness, a shrill yapping sound brought me back to reality. My gorgeous new brother was standing next to the sofa, asking to be lifted up onto it. I guessed his little legs were incapable of propelling him to such heights. Katia reached down and plucked him from the floor. She placed him on her lap, and started to tickle him under the ears. I didn't mind. If I'd been given any more love I was worried my contentment might just overflow.

Pooch

I checked carefully all around me. No other dogs were getting hugs. It was just me. Suddenly I felt better; the world was coming to its senses. But my monopoly on the supply of human affection did not last. The doorbell rang, and I had no option other than to jump off Katia's lap and sprint to the front door, yapping maniacally. The other dogs paid no attention to the bell. They were ignorant. They didn't know what dogs were supposed to do when that noise occurred. Again my superiority shone through.

Stewart opened the door to let in my grandparents. They had come to visit me! I was ecstatic to see them. I jumped at their knees to greet them and tried my best to trip them up by running in circles as they walked into the living room. Then there was an eruption of excitement from the other dogs, which was peculiar because they were *my* grandparents. They were obviously here to see me. There was no reason for any other dog to be pleased to see them.

Then the situation became odder. Instead of picking me up and kissing the suspiciously stinky whiskers on my face, like they were supposed to do, they ignored me and walked over to the corner of the living room where the naughty puppies were incarcerated behind pieces of furniture. Why would they want to look at puppies instead of me? It made no logical sense at all. Stewart bent over a chest of drawers and picked up the muckiest of all the pups. His thick fur was matted with everything imaginable (not Stewart's, I meant the puppy's), and his daft little eyes peeped out through this dense carpet of grossness.

'This is the one they called Foam at the shelter,' he said. 'Horrible name. Symptom of rabies. I'm sure you can do better.'

He put Foam into my grandmother's arms, just like he should have been doing with me. My grandmother was oblivious to the dog's foul odours. I suppose she had developed some level of immunity from being with me. She held him tight and kissed him.

'I'm going to change his name,' she said. 'Foam is silly. So I'll call him Biscuit.'

If I had been drinking I would have choked on my water. Biscuit? In what way was that not silly? Why couldn't he be called something sensible like Pooch? He didn't look like a biscuit, and he certainly wouldn't taste as good as one. And in any case, what was this obsession with a stray puppy anyway? Why was no one talking about me anymore? Hello? Is anyone even listening to me? HELLO!

Mary

Pitz was doing a little dance. It was very sweet to watch, but I think I was the only one who noticed it. Besides, I was more interested in watching my puppy, now called Biscuit (which I thought was a thoroughly dignified and grandiose name), relaxing in the arms of the new visitors to the house. It seemed they were going to be his new family. My little boy was officially rescued. I was so proud of him. They took him with them later that day, off to begin his new career as a pampered pet. He was going to have a life of indulgence and love. I couldn't have asked for anything more. If we had still been living rough in Greece I might not have been able to offer him a life at all. This was a great moment.

During the next few days I settled into my new home, respectfully and cautiously exploring the rooms, only venturing upstairs if invited, sniffing in wide-nosed wonder at the fabulous things I found: aromatic soft rugs; big whiffy cushions; fascinatingly stinky doormats. More visitors arrived. A woman and her adorable children came to adopt Sara, my only little girl, and decided to rename her Zorba. They played together and bonded in the garden, and Zorba didn't look back as she trotted off to their car to begin her new adventure. The next day another lady came to adopt Alfie, and she seemed happy to keep his name. My last puppy, Shadow, was adopted by a woman who renamed him Casper. She also decided to give a place in her home and her heart to my shy friend Hermes the Husky, who had spent most of his time hiding beneath the coffee table in the living room since his arrival.

It was a gradual process, but eventually Pitz and I were the only two dogs remaining in the house. I hoped no one would come to take either of us away. I was happy here, and I loved having Pitz around.

Pooch

One by one the creatures who had invaded my home departed. Each time one of the dogs was adopted, I kept my distance. I didn't say goodbye to them, and they said nothing to me. They were too consumed in the apparent excitement of going to live with a new family to think about me. And I couldn't have cared less, in any case. They had no right to live with me, and I was tired of having to share my vast back garden and my infinite supply of healthy and delicious doggy food with them. And yet I was unhappy. For no logical reason, the departures of Biscuit, Zorba, Alfie, Casper and Hermes left me with an uncomfortable feeling of emptiness. Obviously I didn't miss them, and was glad to see them go, but at the same time I couldn't shake that feeling of hollowness. Evidently there was something wrong with me, and I felt sure that this mysterious minor ailment would soon pass.

Within days I was back to my normal, irresistible self – yapping, peeing, making a mess and constantly demanding attention. One evening at meal time, I turned my nose up at the food in my little bowl and shoved my nose into Mary's bowl. She weighed four times as much me, so her bowl was correspondingly more capacious and so was her food allowance. I sniffed in awe at the mountain of doggy food before me. Mary stood back, politely giving me the space to steal her dinner. She showed no aggression or frustration, only love and consideration. What an odd animal, I thought to myself. After some moments I concluded that I wouldn't be able to finish her food for her, and returned to my own bowl. Mary waited to make sure that was what I wanted before she commenced her eating. She knew I was top dog and was making it easy for me to remain so. Too easy, in fact. Her gentle respect and selflessness made me feel almost, I don't know, guilty? Yes, that's the word. Guilty.

I was unfamiliar with this feeling. I didn't know what it was for. I hoped it would go away.

The next day Stewart threw a toy rabbit in the living room. It landed between me and Mary. We both instinctively dived towards the bunny, but when Mary saw that I was trying to fetch it as well she stepped back and let me take it. What was she doing? We were supposed to fight for it. I expected to have to snap and snarl at her until she ran away with her tail between her legs, but she slickly avoided such a confrontation. She was messing with my mind. She was displaying a generosity of character that deepened my sense of guilt even further. I dropped the toy. If there was no competition for it, I didn't want it. She then picked it up and played with it. I watched her throw the rabbit mindlessly around the room. It was one of my oldest toys, recently reduced to a hollow bag of synthetic fur with a missing ear. I continued to witness the ongoing destruction of this rabbit and realised something peculiar.

I didn't mind.

There was definitely something wrong with me. This was a recurrence of the inexplicable symptoms I'd felt the previous day, a kind of indifference verging almost on affection towards another animal. I shook my head to clear it of these impure thoughts. Mary was my enemy. She did not belong here. I would not be defeated in this battle to reclaim my dominion.

I managed to spend the rest of the day on my own. Mary was sunbathing in the garden and I snoozed in my bed most of the time. Katia and Stewart were doing some DIY in the utility room, ripping out an old sink and radiator to make room for a washing machine or something. They were making unpleasant noises with spanners and hammers and drills, and eventually I got so fed up with having my important afternoon siesta continually interrupted that I decided to go and complain. Mary trotted in from the garden as I emerged from my bed, and she followed me to the utility room as I prepared to deliver my formal protest.

But Katia and Stewart didn't notice me. For some reason, they only saw Mary and decided to take a break from their plumbing work in order to play with my big sister in the garden. The three of them ran through the kitchen and went outside, shouting and laughing. I stood in the utility room admiring the mess. There were tools everywhere. The dirty floor was wet where they had just disconnected a sink and sealed the old water supply pipe. But I don't think they'd done a great job, because the pipe was leaking. Water was dribbling down to the ground, and the rate of flow seemed to be increasing as the temporary seal weakened further. Then a gust of wind blew through the slightly-open window and caused the window to close and the door to slam shut.

I was trapped. This was a tiny room, and the water was spreading all over the floor. It had nowhere to go and it started to rise. I panicked. I wasn't ready for a bath. My next bathing event wasn't booked until July. And as the water enveloped my feet I realised this was it. I might not only have to endure an unscheduled bath, I also might not make it out of here. I was going to drown, and no one

would hear my final yapping bark because they were
too busy playing in the garden.

Mary

I loved to play with the ball. It bounced like it was alive, and when Stewart threw it over my head directly to Katia I jumped and chased and sneezed with happiness, even though I didn't actually catch it. I was rubbish at catching balls, to be honest. You need two eyes to be good at that sort of thing. I wasn't far off having the right number of ocular organs, being deficient only to the tune of one, but it still wasn't enough. Katia and Stewart were laughing loudly as they teased me, but above their noises I heard something else. A dog was barking. It was a muffled sound, but it had a tone that I knew all too well. It was the sound of a dog in distress. In Greece this had been a familiar part of the aural landscape, and there was nothing the other dogs could do about it, but in my new home it was something I had not heard before, and now, I realised, things were different. There *was* something I could do about it. I ran to Katia and Stewart and started whining.

'What's wrong, Mary?' asked Katia.

I continued to whine.

'She never whines like that,' said Stewart. 'There must be something wrong. What is it, Mary?'

I led the way back into the house. I knew the animal in distress was my baby brother. Once indoors my new humans could hear it, too. I ran to the utility room and stood there, still whining loudly, as they opened the door. A couple of centimetres of water rushed out, and a soggy and sorry-looking Pitz stood in the middle of the room, shivering. Katia picked him up in her arms while Stewart attended to the plumbing mishap by throwing towels all over the floor and then phoning an actual plumber to come and do the work properly.

As Pitz was carried past me, he gave me a look that I hadn't seen on his face before. It was a subtle expression, one that only another dog could recognise, but I understood it perfectly. It was a look of gratitude. It was almost as if he was looking at me with a twinkle in his eye. I grinned back at him before helping to clean up the mess by drinking some of the flood water.

Pooch

Some days after the flood incident, my grandparents paid another visit, bringing Biscuit with them. Biscuit immediately began to play with Mary, and they ran outside and chased each other around the lawn. When they came back inside, panting and dribbling, I intended to snap at them as they went past me. An appropriate expression of my disapproval and grumpiness was my plan, but when the moment came I found myself getting swept up in the fun of the occasion and joining in with their games. What was wrong with me?

As if that wasn't strange enough, I found myself feeling concerned later that week when Mary was whisked off to the vet's and didn't come back. What had happened to her? I walked around the garden sniffing where she had peed, picking up toys she had played with and feeling a sense of emptiness without her there. What was going on in my head? Why would I care about another animal?

I think that was when I realised something profound. Mary was now part of my family. She was a good dog. She was respectful and considerate towards me. At times I even thought she fancied me, which would not be surprising as I'm incredibly handsome and about as manly as a thirty-centimetre-tall creature can be. I'd witnessed the poverty from which she and her puppies had been rescued, and I began to feel a sense of pride at my bold and noble decision to emancipate them from their tragic origins. My decision to adopt Mary had been risky, and had come at considerable expense to my toys and my garden, but now that she had settled into my family I knew it had been the right thing to do. Mary brought sunshine into our lives. My generous, selfless rescue mission to Greece had reduced the suffering in the world, albeit by just a small amount, but I had done it. I had changed the world for the better. I had left my mark, and now I felt on top of the world.

That night Mary was still absent. I couldn't sleep. I worried that I might never see her again. In the morning I woke the household up at dawn and peed quite close to the wee-wee pad near the back door. Some of my spray even made it onto the absorbent cloth, but there was no time to feel proud of my target practice. I was concerned for the missing Mary. I was her brother and it was my duty to take care of her, and that was something at which I had spectacularly failed. I spent hours restlessly pacing about the house, sniffing the ubiquitous clumps of Mary's fur that threatened to turn the wooden floor into a carpet. At lunchtime my fears morphed into hilarity when Mary staggered in through the front door with her head wedged in a lampshade. I was mightily relieved to see her, despite her ridiculous appearance, but of course I played it cool and didn't show any affection because that's the kind of dude I am.

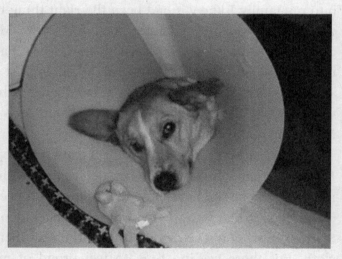

Mary staggered in through the front door with her head wedged in a lampshade.

Mary

From the moment I woke up that morning I felt very peculiar. I was sleepy and dizzy and numb. And I couldn't lick myself because I had somehow grown a plastic cone around my head during my night at the vet's. Stewart and Katia collected me soon after I woke up and carried me to their car, pausing briefly to permit me to wee on the lawn outside the surgery. Squatting felt painful. I almost fell down on the grass. Everything was confusing. When I arrived home – and, by the way, even in my spaced-out state I was still grateful that the word 'home' was something I could use – I tried to walk into the house, but my cone hit the door frame and knocked me backwards. Then my little brother Pitz appeared, saw me, and ran around in excited circles, yapping and smiling. He came up and sniffed all around me, and even managed to put his face inside the cone to lick my nose affectionately. I had never known such an openly warm and loving welcome, but I was tired, and when Stewart carried me to my bed I was grateful for the opportunity to fall into a deep sleep.

When finally I awoke, with a neck that felt stiff from having that strange cone around it, I sensed something warm lying up against me. I couldn't turn my head far enough to see what it was, but it was breathing and it was snoring. I inhaled its odours through my nose and realised that Pitz was cuddled up against me, sharing my bed. There was a dull and throbbing pain in my abdomen from where the vet had mended me (I think I needed to be cured of the disease of having more puppies or something), but that pain soon receded beneath the wave of elation that swept through me. Pitz was taking care of me during my recovery. It was the sweetest thing another dog had ever done for me.

Pooch

My big, baby sister wore that lampshade on her head for a week while I nursed her back to health. I made sure she stayed warm and comfortable, which also had the effect of keeping me rather cosy at the same time. We had become more than friends. This stray animal, who had once had nothing, had become part of my family. Not the best part, because that's me, obviously, but with nothing more than her charming and loving nature she had secured a better life for herself and her puppies and I thought that was pretty amazing. I never would have believed that I could find the company of another dog enjoyable. I used to worry that another dog in the house meant less food for me, fewer toys, less affection – but it's worked out just fine. Somehow, as if by magic, there was always enough food for both of us. There were now more toys than I used to have. And the humans seemed to love us both. I had risked everything to adopt Mary, and the gamble had paid off. Would I do it again, though? I wasn't sure about that. I had done my bit for society. So when a frightened Beagle called Brando arrived at our house, I was surprised to encounter a weird emotion in my little head. I was actually pleased to see him.

We had become more than friends.

Brando

Is it my turn now? Oh no! I'm not ready! Can I come back later? Oh, the book's nearly over, is it? I suppose I'd better tell my story then. It's a bit painful to think back to my time in Greece. I feel sick in my stomach when I recall the science laboratory. I don't need to spell it out, do I? You know the kind of place I'm talking about. Beagles, monkeys, rats, all in little cages, all being injected with experimental drugs and subjected to painful blood tests and other undignified examinations. We were all terrified. I was probably more scared than any of them. One morning I woke up with bandages on my chest. Blood soaked through and stained the floor of my cage. I'll never know what they did to me, and the scars are mostly hidden now that the fur has regrown, but I sat and shivered with fear for days after that.

The Beagles in the lab would sometimes be taken away, never to be seen again. There were rumours about them being killed when their experiments were finished, and a fresh puppy would then take their place. So when the time came for me to be plucked from my cage, I guessed the end was near. I wasn't even a year old and I had never seen daylight.

I had lived in misery for the whole of my short life. I didn't try to resist or defend myself: I was too distressed to function properly. A human wearing a mask gently lifted me up and carried me out of the lab. It was dark outside, and all I remember is a long car journey which ended at a gate. A collar was placed around my neck, and a rope was then used to attach me to this gate. The masked human disappeared. I sat, shivering in the cool night air, waiting for something bad to happen.

It did. Something huge and yellow started to rise into the sky. I cowered, but there was nowhere to hide. I had never seen anything like it before. I felt hot and thirsty. Insects crawled over me. Birds swooped menacingly above me. And, not far away, came the voices of incarcerated dogs. A human appeared and disconnected me from the gate, looked around, then led me towards the source of the barking. I had arrived at a place known as Skiathos Dog Shelter, but my journey towards freedom was far from over. A few weeks later I was put in a portable crate and loaded into a van. I spent days in this van, stacked up with crates containing other dogs, while we journeyed across Europe, stopping only to pee occasionally. The whole experience was so upsetting that I kept my eyes closed for much of the trip. I still didn't know if this was part of the process of killing off former laboratory dogs. Every time I peed I wondered if it was my last.

We arrived at a farm in a cold country called England. Behind the farmhouse was something that looked like another dog shelter. I was put into a bare cell. It was noisy here: the steel doors banged and the dogs barked. It was too much for me. I had no escape from the terror that engulfed me and I started to shut down internally. I curled up in the corner of my cell and tried to block out the world – I've had some pretty deep lows in my time, but this was the deepest of all – and that was when a scary woman walked into the compound. And by scary, I mean petrifying. I didn't like people at all. Especially when they moved or made a noise or sneezed or breathed. I couldn't cope with their movements and sounds. It triggered too many flashbacks of the scientists in the laboratory. So when this lady walked into the yard, I hid further at the back of my cage than ever before. The monstrous human approached the door of my cell and tried to look at me. I shrank inside myself, hoping she wouldn't spot me, but she opened the door. It was a horrendous moment. A Beagle should not be subjected to this kind of abuse. I shivered and closed my eyes, hoping the world would go away if I ignored it.

'Hello Brando,' said the woman. 'I'm Katia. Would you like to come home with me to meet my doggies?'

I don't know why she was talking to me. I'm just a dog. I couldn't even speak a word of English. And it wasn't as if I had any choice in the matter, anyway. She put a lead on me and took me to her car. An hour later I met Mary and Pitz. I was supposed to live with them for a week, just until I found a family to adopt me. And five years later I'm still living with them. It turned out that I was so fearful and screwed-up that no-one wanted to adopt me. The psychological damage done to me during my formative months was so severe that even after I moved in with Mary and Pitz and their humans, it took six months before I smiled, nine months before I wagged my tail (up to that point my humans wondered if it was broken), a year before I worked out what a ball was for, and a further six months before I plucked up the courage to play with Mary in the garden. I'll always have a nervous disposition, I suppose, but living with a family has given me the strength and courage that I never thought possible. I've learned how to have fun. I now wag my tail every day. I smile when I recognise someone. I often have bad dreams about my old life, but things are good now. I enjoy my life. I'm glad I was rescued.

I'm glad I was rescued.

Mary

Ah, he's adorable, isn't he? I love my new brother Brando. We don't talk much about our pasts in Greece. To be honest, I think we've both forgotten how to bark the language. Now that we have learned a few words of English there's not much room in our brains for a vestigial language for which we have no further use. When I say 'we', I have to be honest and say that I'm being generous by including Brando in the category of having learned English. He doesn't really respond to any words, English or otherwise, apart from his name, and even then he has to spend a minute or two thinking about it before making the connection. It's fair to say he's not the brightest star in the firmament, but I love him and I feel very protective about him.

I tried to teach him how to chase cats, but they ended up chasing him. I tried showing him how to play with cuddly toys, but he found the experience rather stressful. Katia is always saying there's something special about him. I never quite understand what she means, but it's something to do with his knees, apparently. Brando has special knees. Yes, that's what it is. He's a special knees dog.

Though, to be honest, I've seen his knees many times and they look quite unremarkable to me.

Brando possesses the purest heart I've ever known. He knows nothing of aggression or selfishness, only a desire to feel safe and to be loved. Well, he has both those things now, and I will make sure that nothing changes. He'll always be nervous and retiring – if he was a snail he'd spend all his time inside his shell, and that's not good because how would the shell ever get cleaned? I make an effort to bring him out of his shell – actually his doggy bed – every day, but I always take care not to damage his knees, knowing, as I do, how special they are.

He's a special knees dog.

Pooch

But not as special as *my* knees, and every other part
of me. Brando was a walkover. Easily dominated.
Instantly knew I was in charge and kept himself a
safe distance from me. He never touched my food or
my toys. Never spoke to me. Never tried to play with
me. I liked him.

It was a bad day when he ran away. A dropped
lead just at the end of a walkies scared him and he
bolted. Just ran and ran and ran. His lead dragged
behind him, making a noise which terrified him, so
he kept running from that noise. No one could keep
up with him. I insisted that a search party be
organised as soon as my dinner had been served to
my satisfaction. I sent it back the first time, because
there wasn't enough cheese on top, but after that I
ate it, and then authorised the search to begin.
Though my instructions must have been lost in
translation because half the population of the town
were already out looking for Brando.

I helped with the design and printing of dozens of
'lost dog' posters. And by 'help' I mean I didn't
hinder the process in any way, apart from the
occasional demand for attention and cuddles. I
oversaw the writing of e-mails to the press, radio

stations, scout groups, lost dog websites and rambling groups. I assisted in numerous drives and walks around the town, putting up posters and searching behind bushes for the elusive Brando. Days passed. There was no sign of him. I considered the possibility that he had gone back to Greece, but I don't think he knew the way.

Then a phone call – someone ringing to ask if we'd found him. Not much help. The next call did help, however. The errant Beagle had been spotted several miles from where he had begun his silly journey. The search now focused on the farms in that area. It was April and the rain hammered down relentlessly. I don't do walkies in the rain. There's no point. I decided that Mary should take over the responsibility for the search.

Mary

Poor Brando, out in the rain, cold and frightened and hungry. I knew how that felt, and I was determined that we would find him. Every day I took the humans out into the country to walk for miles and miles, searching the fields and paths and farm buildings for any sign of Brando. A week passed, and we had only received one sighting. Was he still in that area? Were we looking in the wrong place? More posters went up, more reports put out on local radio, more people joined the search, and I was at the heart of it, using my finely-tuned nose to sniff out any traces of my shy brother.

Another phone call reached us, this time from a man who seemed very angry. He was calling from a small aerodrome. A pilot. He had been forced to abandon his take-off because a Beagle had just run across his runway. He'd tried chasing the dog, but it had got away. Oh dear, I thought. Brando was getting into deep trouble.

We narrowed our search to the perimeter of the aerodrome. The rain came down hard, all day long, as we searched every inch of the vast site. I thought I could smell him, but the scent was old, fading. Brando wasn't there any longer.

I missed him most at night. I had got used to hearing him snoring in his bed next to mine. He would snuffle and shake when his dreams became intense. Good dreams would make his tail wag; bad ones would cause him to wake up with a look of panic in his big eyes. Then he would see that I was there for him and he would relax and go back to sleep and the snoring would begin again. Nights weren't the same without that reassuring drone from his little nose.

Two days later came a report from an adjoining farm that Brando had been seen several times running in and out of a field of wheat. We enlisted the council dog warden who set a trail of food leading to a large cage with a trap door. The warden advised us not to visit the cage until the next morning, in order not to frighten Brando. He would be starving by now, and would be sure to follow the trail of food. I agreed. I knew what it was like to spend more than a week without eating. It wasn't something I would wish on any dog.

The next morning the food was gone, except for what was in the bowl inside the cage. If Brando wanted to eat again, he would have to find the courage to step inside that cage and eat the final bowl. We returned home and waited. After dark, I led the way through the fields to the site of the cage.

The trap door was closed. Inside, sitting upright, looking tired and confused, was the most sorry-looking creature I had ever seen. He had lost so much weight, his ribs were showing. He was covered in ticks and fleas. He looked shamed and embarrassed by his foolishness. Katia scooped him into her arms and held him on her lap as we drove home.

Brando's knees became even more special from then on. Stewart bought him a GPS tracking device, so that if he escaped again we could track his location on a smartphone. Brando loves wearing the GPS on his collar. Makes him feel very important. And new procedures for walkies were introduced: Brando must at all times either be clipped to a human or to me. That way, if the lead were to be dropped, he couldn't run off. I'm not daft enough to run away, so if he's clipped to me he won't be going anywhere. And now we have a double-ended lead, attached to both of us. That's how we take humans for a walk, by letting them hold it in the middle. I know it's a bit odd, but the humans seem to like it, except when we get engrossed in a good sniff and walk in alternating circles, twisting the lead around the human's legs so they can't walk.

Brando

Mary asked me to write my account of my time in the wilderness. I told her I didn't want to, but she said I could make it short. So this is what happened during my ten lost days. Scared, tired, cold, wet, hungry, bleeding, exhausted, freezing, terrified, shivering, lonely, chased, cowering, starving. Night after night. Horror after horror. Endless rain soaking my shrinking body, ticks chomping, stomach rumbling. Then food. Then a cage. More food. Cage door slammed. Katia. Cuddles. All good.

Mary

It was strange, at first, to live with humans. Their habits are inexplicable. For example, they scrape seemingly good food into a bin and never take it back out to eat it, whereas for me it was always the other way round. But despite this culture clash I know I'm a lucky dog. I never forget that. Each morning when I wake up, I'm so happy to realise I no longer have to cower under a wheelie bin. I no longer face starvation. My life has changed and I now have everything I ever dreamed of: a home; bounteous food and water; all the toys I can eat; a secure garden; regular walkies; a family to love me; a vet to cure me; and my brother Pitz who adores me (even if he's too macho to show it). And now there's also my latest brother, Brando. He's struggled to cope since he was rescued from that laboratory, but I'm helping to teach him how to play, how to chase cats, how to sneak up onto the sofa, and how to get cuddles from humans. He's very shy and rather a slow learner, but he'll get there. Last week I saw him pick up a stuffed toy and play with it for a few seconds. That was a major break-through. Then he smiled at me. I love to see him smile. Now that he's not afraid of toys, he can really start to have fun.

I now have everything I ever dreamed of.

I am also fortunate that I get to see my puppies occasionally. When they visit with their new owners we play and play and play and play until we collapse, exhausted, on the shredded lawn. And then we get up and play some more. They are so big now that it's hard to tell them when to stop: I can't pick them up and put them to one side like I used to when they were tiny. I love to see them happy with their new families, and I'm so proud that I was able to bring them with me to a country where no dogs are allowed to go hungry.

Despite my blissful existence, deep inside of me lurks a pain. It is a memory, admittedly one that grows weaker by the year, of the dogs I left behind in Greece. Friends, acquaintances, familiar faces and smells – it has been six years since I saw them. I doubt that more than a pawful of them made it through the first winter after my rescue – by now it's probable that none of my community remains – but some will have had puppies, and some of those puppies might have survived. A group of homeless hounds will still be living in Orei, consisting of the children and grandchildren of those I used to know, all of them with empty stomachs, all of them scared and lonely, all of them dreaming that perhaps one day a family will arrive to pluck them from misery and take them to a better world.

The tragic thing is that most of them won't live to see such a day.

I may only be a dog, but I know a thing or two. I've heard about puppy farms. I've heard about dog breeders and pet shops that sell puppies – a huge industry, dedicated to creating new dogs for people to buy and take home. But isn't there something wrong with that?

Let me try to explain. According to Katia, who can count a lot higher than I can, there are as many as two hundred million dogs (apparently that's a lot) scratching a meagre and unhappy existence on the streets of the world. Two hundred million doggy souls, all starving, all lonely, all yearning for comfort and companionship and shelter, all capable of giving love and affection to humans if permitted the chance. So why are people deliberately breeding new dogs before rescuing the ones already out there? I don't understand it.

Katia says there are more homes with gardens in the wealthy nations of the world than there are stray dogs. I didn't ask if she had counted them, but I trust her. She thinks there is no need for any dog to remain homeless, and I agree. If every family adopted and neutered one lost hound the problem would be solved in an instant. Imagine the joy I felt – and continue to feel – about my rescue, and then multiply that joy by two hundred million times.

Can you imagine that much happiness? Is that the kind of world you would like to live in? I know I would.

Pooch

With Brando settled as part of the household, albeit at the bottom end of the pecking order (situated beneath me, Mary, the earwig under the skirting board and the squashed snail on the doorstep) we became a happy family.

With Brando settled as part of the household, albeit at the bottom end of the pecking order (situated beneath me, Mary, the earwig under the skirting board and the squashed snail on the doorstep) we became a happy family.

We made frequent trips to my holiday home in Spain, always travelling by car: Mary and Brando had the back seat, and I had Katia's lap.

We would stop off at a motel in France to break the journey, and Stewart would smuggle us hounds into the room when he was sure no one from the motel's management was looking. The entire canine contingent would then try to keep Stewart awake all night by snoring loudly enough to render him insufficiently rested for the next day's drive.

There was a dog shelter near my Spanish home. Katia volunteered to help them when she was there. She was, admittedly, quite expert at picking up poo, but she also started to assist the vets who came to treat the unwanted mutts. She took part in neutering operations –unlike normal people, she didn't pass out at the sight of a scalpel or blood. She discovered a passion for surgery. She decided she wanted to become a vet.

Now, I always knew Katia was smart: she can open doors, she can turn on lights, she can put doggy food in my bowl and scrape it into the bin after I've refused to eat it – that takes the kind of brains I can't even imagine. But becoming a vet requires intellect on a whole new level. There would be books and lectures and student life and lots of partying. It was a big commitment. Animals in the future would benefit from her ambition, but would it affect me in the short term? I became profoundly concerned at this possibility until I fell asleep and forgot all about it.

Katia was accepted by the University of Surrey to pursue her veterinary degree. That meant moving house. And a new house meant new sniffs and lots of packing materials to play with. That was good.

'Shall we get pet insurance?' I heard Katia asking as we settled into our new home. A Victorian cottage, formerly inhabited by the head teacher of the village school along with his family, his servants, and hordes of delicious mice. I could smell them everywhere. The mice, not the Victorian servants. I think.

'Don't be daft,' came Stewart's sensible reply. 'You're going to be a vet in a few years. You can treat them yourself!'

She nodded in agreement before returning to the more pressing matter of picking me up and giving me an overdue cuddle. Over the next few weeks we made the cottage our own. Katia put up paintings and photos, including a framed set of pictures of Mary and her four silly offspring which she hung above the fireplace, presumably as a warning to Father Christmas to keep away. Stewart tackled the overgrown garden, and I contributed in my own special way by peeing on the carpets and forcing Stewart to abandon the gardening efforts and focus instead on ripping out all the old carpets and underlay, which apparently were starting to stink like a public toilet. What did he expect? It was too much for me to bother going outside to pee at my venerable age. So now we had bare floorboards, and the winter winds blew into the house. My elderly joints became stiffer. The antique heating system struggled to cope. Once the chimney was swept we started using the fireplace in the living room and I would put my bed in front of it and gaze contentedly into the hypnotic flames for hours on end, musing about how great I am.

Mary

He is great, isn't he? It's a shame he was getting too slow to come for walkies anymore. He barely even used the new garden. His ears didn't work too well, his eyes had a glaze of grey which made it hard for him to see far beyond the hearth that became his cosy home, and his body grew thinner as his muscles withered in line with his appetite. Stewart and Katia tried to tempt his palette with ever more elaborate meals, but, sadly (though not for me) most of those meals ended up scraped into my bowl or Brando's.

But while little Pooch started to decline, Brando and I were going strong. We settled into a new routine of walkies through the fields of Surrey, making friends with horses and sheep, going for breakfast in the Cyder House pub on Saturday mornings, and loving our village life. Katia had long holidays between university semesters and we would always spend them in Spain. With our second Christmas in Surrey approaching, the conversation turned to when we would make the journey south.

'How about we spend Christmas in Surrey and head to Spain for the New Year?' suggested Stewart.

'I don't know. I've got a lot of studying to do. Maybe we should go later when I've had time to catch up.'

'Can't you study in the car?'

'I get sick.'

'So work hard, and I won't book the Channel Tunnel crossing just yet, but maybe we'll go sometime between Boxing Day and New Year's Eve? The house in Spain needs urgent repairs. We can't leave it much longer.'

Boxing Day came. We didn't travel. More days passed by, and still we were in Surrey. It wasn't so bad. While Katia studied the instruction manuals for dogs and cats and horses and sheep, Brando and I took Stewart on long walkies every afternoon before the feeble December sun slunk behind the horizon, and we'd spend evenings by the fire watching the Christmas specials on television.

By New Year's Eve it was obvious we weren't going to Spain any time soon. That afternoon I connected myself to Brando, as usual, and took Stewart for another long walk. I was energetic, strong, and full of beans. The walk was muddy, requiring two towels to clean us when we got back. I ate my dinner that evening and vomited on the kitchen floor.

'Silly dog,' said Stewart, cleaning up the steaming heap of undigested food from the tiles. 'Katia, are you done studying for today? Shall we go to the pub?'

'Nowhere near done, but I really want a drink.'

'So stop. It's New Year's Eve. Let's go out.'

But she didn't stop, and they didn't go out. If they had done, I would have died before they returned.

Pooch

Mary smelled funny. It takes a dog to notice this stuff. And even though I am permanently engulfed in my own miasma of canine odours, I could tell something was amiss with my adopted sister. Even through the smell of her puke, and even through the citron freshness of the disinfectant used to clean it up, a concerning smell floated from Mary into my nose. It had its own wavelength, invisible to humans, but to a dog's finely-tuned nostrils it was a clear signature of something bad.

I also noticed Mary's tail started to droop. For the world's most optimistic dog, this was unheard of. She lay down on the living room floor, close to me. Her belly was swollen.

'Probably needs a poo,' said Stewart, guiding Mary to the back door. 'Or a fart. Either way, she's going outside.'

Mary walked slowly, lacking the enthusiasm she normally displayed for such exciting events as a visit to the garden. Outside was freezing. She didn't return quickly. Stewart went to look.

'She's lying down outside!' he shouted.

Katia ran to the window. This was odd behaviour. Katia never ran. And Mary never usually lay down outside in the cold.

'Bring her in,' said Katia. 'Let me take a look at her.'

Stewart guided Mary back through the kitchen and into the warmth of the living room. Mary flopped to the floor, seemingly exhausted by the short walk indoors. Her belly was even larger than it had been ten minutes before.

'Perhaps she needs to be sick again?' Stewart suggested. He knew a good spew fixed most doggy ailments.

'I'm not sure,' said Katia. 'I've never seen anything like this before.'

'She was fine this afternoon,' Stewart continued. 'Dragged me and Brando through the woods with her usual energy. Must be a bit of food poisoning. Let's go to the pub, and if she's still iffy tomorrow, we'll call the vet.'

Katia examined Mary more closely. She looked worried.

'I don't know what's wrong with her. I think we should call the vet now.'

'Are you serious? It's New Year's Eve. It's probably the most expensive time to speak to a vet in the whole year!'

'Just call for advice. I'll do some more checks on her.'

Stewart looked up the number and dialled it. Mary lay still and listless as Katia checked her over. Stewart had a short conversation and hung up.

'What did they say?' Katia asked.

'It's out of hours, so a consultation will cost £250.'

'Really? Do they think we need one?'

'Hopefully not. It wasn't a vet that I spoke to, just an assistant. She's going to call the duty vet and then phone back with advice. I'm sure Mary just needs to do a big poo and she'll be fine. There was nothing wrong with her earlier.'

But Katia had carried out more vet-type examinations on Mary, and suddenly her face fell.

'Call them back!' she yelled. 'Tell them we're coming right now!'

'What? Why? What's happened?'

He fumbled with the buttons on the phone as he tried to redial.

'Get me some honey.'

'This is no time for a sandwich. What's the matter?'

'Look at Mary's gums,' she said, pulling back the dog's lips. The gums were white. 'She's going into shock. This could be serious.'

Stewart ran into the kitchen, dialling the vet's number in one hand and returning with a jar of honey in the other. Katia spread some honey on Mary's lips while Stewart told the vet to prepare for Mary's arrival.

'What's the honey for?'

'It helps bring her out of shock. Come on, get her into the car.'

I decided at this point that I needed to pee. I staggered up with my doddery, withered legs and stumbled towards the kitchen. Normally Stewart would race to the back door and try to open it before I could pee indoors. This time he ignored me. Charming, I thought, as I peed on the kitchen floor, watching it run in the grooves between the tiles, following the slight gradient of the Victorian floor.

Stewart was trying to get Mary to walk to the front door. Normally she would charge at full speed to the door. This time he had to carry her. And that was it. They were gone. Just me and Brando left alone on New Year's Eve. What a party that was going to be, with him hiding in his bed, terrified of the fireworks, and me fast asleep dreaming about sausages.

Mary

I fell unconscious in the car. When I woke up I was in a cold, white room with a needle in my leg connected to a tube. I was weak and in a lot of pain, especially around my bloated stomach. I pointed my eye towards the vet. He was talking to Katia and Stewart. They were trying not to cry.

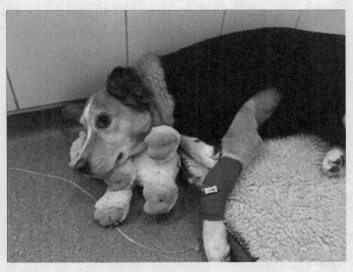

When I woke up I was in a cold, white room with a needle in my leg connected to a tube.

'I've seen this before,' said the vet. 'You did the right thing bringing her in. If it's what I think it is, she would have died within minutes.'

'We thought she needed a poo,' said Stewart, his voice choking as the reality of my situation sank in. 'But you're saying she needs emergency surgery?'

'She does, but it might not help,' he replied. 'Mary has severe internal bleeding. She's lost a lot of blood. That's why she's so weak. The most likely cause is a tumour on her spleen. They grow without any symptoms, and then they burst. I can open her up and remove the spleen and stop the blood loss, but...'

He paused. I closed my eye, but continued listening.

'So you can fix her?' asked Katia.

'It will be £1,500 for the operation,' he said. 'I need to clear that with you first. Does Mary have insurance?'

'No,' Stewart replied, sheepishly, 'but do it, anyway.'

'I can do it, but there are several issues to consider. First, if the cancer has spread to her other organs—'

'What?' Stewart interrupted. 'She has cancer? How can this evolve so quickly from her needing a big poo to having cancer?'

'A tumour is a type of cancer. These types of tumours are quite common, sadly,' the vet continued. 'Once I open her up I'll be able to see if it's spread to her heart or liver. If so, I'm afraid it wouldn't be fair on Mary to wake her up again. I can remove the spleen, but if it's already present on other organs I can't remove them. There would be nothing we could do.'

'The operation is her only chance?' asked Katia.

I opened my eye again. I didn't like the tone of their voices.

'Yes,' said the vet, looking surprisingly unfazed by the prospect that my illness would ruin his New Year celebrations.

If I wasn't already in shock, I would have been by this time. At least, I would if I had really understood everything, which, of course, I didn't, but I can read people's emotions without comprehending their words. Somehow, I'm able to report those incomprehensible words, verbatim, which is lucky, because this book would have been really short otherwise.

'So a tumour that's spread is the worst case scenario,' said Katia. 'What else could it be?'

'If we're lucky, it won't have spread, and it might not be malignant. A benign tumour would be the best outcome, but it's not very likely. Anyway, she's very weak and we need to prep for surgery immediately.'

'Stewart, why don't you pop back home and put the other dogs to bed, and I'll stay here while Mary has her surgery?' suggested Katia.

Stewart nodded and left. The vet approached me with a needle. The pain evaporated and I fell into a deep sleep.

Pooch

It was a couple of hours before midnight when Stewart returned home. He let me and Brando into the garden, and started to clean up my pee-pee in the kitchen. Almost as soon as we had returned to the living room, the phone rang. Stewart answered – well, it works best when he does it; Brando and I are equally useless at working the handset. He even managed to put it on speaker phone so he could continue scrubbing the floor while he spoke.

'So, Mary's still alive. Just.' It was Katia's voice. She sounded concerned, but not about me, which I thought was odd. 'He started the operation, but she's lost a lot more blood than he thought. She really was minutes away from dying.'

'But she's on a drip. She'll get her blood pressure back soon?' asked Stewart.

'No,' Katia replied. 'A saline drip isn't enough. She needs a blood transfusion, but it's impossible. The vet thinks she's not going to make it. We just can't get the supplies from the blood banks. Not now. It's New Year's Eve. Everyone is partying. There's a blood bank up north that's open, but it's an eight-hour round trip. Mary can't wait that long. She'll be dead before the blood arrives. Besides, the vet says she has a rare blood type. It's not something they're likely to have in stock, anyway.'

'There must be something we can do,' said Stewart.

If I could have spoken, I would have generously offered to donate blood. Brando's blood. All of it.

'You should see the vet's face,' said the voice on the phone. 'He really doesn't look hopeful. He's doing his best, but he says we have to face the reality that she won't even see in the New Year.'

'What about Brando? Maybe he's a match? Can he donate blood?'

'I asked that. The vet says there's a limit to how much they can safely extract from each donor dog. He thinks we're going to need four donors. And they have to match Mary's type.'

'The neighbours all have dogs!' said Stewart, as if he'd had a bright idea. 'Why don't I knock on all their doors and ask if they'll help?'

'The blood type. Too rare,' came Katia's reply. 'You could knock on a hundred doors and find only one match. And besides, everyone's out at parties now. It's hopeless. Can you come back here and say goodbye to her?'

Four donor dogs, I thought to myself. I didn't know how many that was, but it was probably more than one. Where had I seen four dogs before? It was a number I was familiar with. I yawned. It was late for me. I considered getting comfortable in my bed in front of the fireplace. This whole drama with Mary was frightening and complicated and maybe if I went to sleep it would all go away by the time I woke up. I tottered towards my bed and glanced at the chimney breast. The framed photos of Mary and her puppies hung above me. All four of her naughty offspring stared out from the wall, their silly doggy faces and delirious smiles brightening the room.

Four puppies. All living with their new families in England. All grown up, now, of course.

I don't know how, but I had an idea. Something connected in my tiny brain in a way that never happened before. It was a brilliant idea; I suddenly realised that if I started to use the rug in the living room as my bathroom I wouldn't have to walk all the way to the kitchen for a pee! This would save me a vast amount of exertion. As I stood still, in stark amazement at my genius, it happened again. Another idea. This time it had nothing to do with my toilet habits. Those puppies in the photos, there were enough of them to save Mary. They were all capable of donating a full serving of doggy blood, all capable of saving their mother's life. They could be the donors we needed, and they would be the right blood group because they were close family. I had done it! I had worked out how to save Mary's life!

I barked at the photo to tell Stewart my plan.

'Shut up, stupid dog.' He picked up his keys and headed for the door, wiping tears from his eyes as he did so.

I barked again and again and again. He knew me well. Something in my tone was different. He turned back, concerned that I was in need of something.

'What is it, Pooch? I have to go. Mary's dying. Hurry up. What's the matter?'

I barked again, trying my best to get him to see the photos on the wall.

'You've got food, you've got water, you've had a pee in the kitchen. There's nothing else. I have to go.'

I gave my all. A final, desperate yap that sent shockwaves down my throat and made my legs wobble.

This time he looked at me, then looked up at the photos on the wall, then looked back at me and smiled.

'Did you really think of that?' he asked, grabbing the phone.

I gave him a dumb smile and settled onto my bed. My work was done.

'Mary's puppies!' he shouted into the phone, excitedly, as if it had been his idea. 'They would be the right blood type, right?' There was a pause. 'I know, I know, but if I phone mum and get her to meet me half way I can collect Biscuit and be back within an hour. The vet can start taking a blood donation from Biscuit while the owners of the other puppies make their way here. Some live further away than others, but by arriving at different times it means we'll have a full portion of blood ready every hour or so, enough to keep it flowing into Mary. Could it work, do you think?' Another pause. 'Yes! Let's do it! I'm going straight to get Biscuit. You call the others. See you in an hour.'

With that he ran out of the door, into the cold night. I went to sleep and dreamed of being a superhero. Which wasn't a dream, really, because I already was one.

Mary

I woke up. That was a good start; I hadn't expected that. But I felt awful. I had tubes and wires sticking out of me. A heart and blood pressure monitor beeped above me. My insides felt like they'd been scooped out with a spoon. I was sick on the floor and struggled to lift my head away from the mess. I passed out again.

Pooch

To honour my selfless heroism, Katia invited me to visit Mary in hospital two days after her operation. Brando was also invited, but he declined the opportunity on account of it being too scary for him. And with Mary in hospital for the foreseeable future, Stewart had popped over to Spain for a few days to do some urgent repairs on my holiday home. So it became my sole responsibility to cheer Mary up with my inspiring and uplifting presence. Piece of cake. Mmm, cake. Lemon drizzle. That would be nice. Or a Battenberg. Not a whole one, obviously. Just a slice. Don't want to be greedy... Where was I? Oh, right. The vet's. Katia carried me through the corridors of the vet's surgery to the intensive care unit. There lay Mary, half dog, half machine. A blood-soaked bandage covered a massive wound across her stomach. A more miserable sight I have never seen in all my seventeen years.

'How's she doing?' Katia asked.

'Blood pressure was rock bottom during the operation,' said the vet. 'Most dogs wouldn't have made it, even with the transfusions. There's something about Mary, though. The transfusion from Biscuit came just in time to keep her from the precipice, and as the other blood donations arrived during the night from her other puppies she gained enough strength to pull through. She's not out of danger yet, but if she carries on this way she'll recover. Those puppies of hers were true heroes. It was so lucky you brought them all back from Greece.'

Ahem, I tried to say. If anyone was a hero, I think it was me. How could they forget so quickly?

'So if she makes a recovery from the operation, what's next for her?' asked Katia.

'We've sent a biopsy of the tumour for examination. That will confirm if it's malignant. And if it is, she's unlikely to make it beyond another three months.'

Katia gulped, and steadied herself before continuing.

'Is there anything we can do?'

'With chemotherapy treatment, she might make it to six months, but she's not insured and each chemo session costs about £600. So you'll have to think carefully about that, because she'll need four of them.'

'Where are we with the bill so far?'

'About £1,500 for the surgery, then it's about £1,000 a day for the intensive care. It will be a week or so before she's ready to come home.'

Mary looked at me, a vague hint of recognition in her eye, and waggled her tail weakly.

'It doesn't matter,' said Katia, looking at the interaction between us. 'Mary trusts us. We'll never let her down.'

At home that evening, I overheard a Skype conversation.

'How much?' asked Stewart.

'It's not about the money,' said Katia.

'No, no, you're right. Of course. But seriously, is it *that* much?'

'I'm going to do some research. There might be a treatment programme we can try. Something new from one of the universities. The vet said he'll also look into other options. We're not giving up on her.'

Over the next few days Katia did just that. She read scientific papers and books. She learned everything she could about Mary's disease. She made daily visits to Mary's intensive care bed, returning each time with a look of concern. Mary was getting thinner, she explained. She had lost her appetite. Any food that went in came straight out again. It was jeopardising her recovery. Stewart rushed home after just three days in Spain. He'd fixed the leaking roof, chiselled open the jammed door and redecorated where the paint had peeled. Now his only concern was Mary's recovery.

'I found a report of a medical trial in Italy,' Katia told him. 'Instead of four chemo treatments they did six, and then followed it up with a monthly dosage of an anti-cancer drug.'

'Did it work?' he asked.

'It wasn't a big trial,' she answered, 'but some of the dogs lasted one, two, even three years after their initial diagnosis. Some of them were still alive when the paper was published.'

'That's a lot better than the three to six months the vet told us.'

'I'll send the paper to him. But Mary has to get stronger before she can start chemotherapy. They've put her on a special medication to help her keep her food down. Unless she recovers her appetite she'll be too weak. And then there'll be no hope.'

Mary

My time in hospital seemed to drag on forever. I had my toys and my smelly blanket for comfort, and Katia visited every afternoon, sometimes with Pooch and sometimes with Stewart, and the nurses gave me cuddles and I made friends with some of the other sick dogs around me, but I felt so strange inside that I couldn't eat. It wasn't that I didn't want to eat. Food was still tempting and taunting to my nose and my eye, but my stomach felt disconnected from those senses. Anything I swallowed came right back. And more than anything, I wanted to go home. I wasn't homeless any more. My life had changed. In Greece I'd had nothing, and so I'd had nothing to lose and nothing to miss. Now I had a family, and my family was everything. I missed them so much. I didn't know it was possible to miss things so badly. I think it was this determination to get back home that forced me to keep trying with the food problem. And after a week, I finally managed to eat a little bowl of chicken and keep it down. I looked at the veterinary nurse: she watched proudly as I finished my meal. I waggled my tail and smiled at her. She could see I was getting stronger. I waggled my tail so hard it shook the stitches in my stomach. This was my ticket out of here.

Later that day, Katia and Stewart arrived holding my lead. The vet handed Katia boxes of medicines, handed Stewart the bill, then handed him a tissue to wipe his eyes as he realised how much it had cost to save my life. When the finances were settled, they took me outside for a pee, lifted me into the car, and brought me home. Home to Brando and Pooch and all the comforting smells and stains that signified to me that I was where I belonged. Katia lit a fire and put me on the sofa. Lifting me was easy for her: I had lost a quarter of my body weight. I settled next to her, struggling to believe my luck. I wasn't normally allowed on the sofa. This was a special moment. While Stewart climbed into the loft looking for things to sell, I put my head on Katia's lap, hoping this moment would last for ever.

Pooch

Mary was spoiled rotten when she came home from the menders. She was allowed on the sofas and on the beds, she was given special food, new toys, and even more cuddles than ever before. The younger me would have been jealous and resentful of this. She was getting far more attention than I was, and it was blatantly unfair that I should be neglected for up to eighteen hours a day, even though I was asleep for more than twenty hours a day. But I understood Mary's needs. She had been through something horrible, and she had a long road to recovery ahead of her. No, I wasn't jealous at all. I was proud to have her as my sister. Proud of her resilience. And proud that she never once complained about her situation.

Every day, Mary's health improved. She moved with greater ease, was less bothered by her stitches and by the shaved patches on her legs where tubes had been inserted, and she ate more voraciously. She took Stewart and Brando on short walks at first, then on longer ones. She even started playing with my toys again.

A month later, when Mary had regained enough strength, she began her chemotherapy treatment, waggling her tail excitedly as she headed off to spend a day at the vet's having nasty drugs pumped into her. She returned, hours later, still full of enthusiasm, grinning as if she'd spent the day at doggy day-care rather than in hospital. Katia had some paperwork in her hand, and showed it to Stewart.

'They tested Mary's heart and blood, and she's fine to do the six chemo sessions,' she said. 'The chemo needs to happen every three weeks. After that is when the monthly cancer drugs start. But there's a problem. This trial is from Italy. The drug they used isn't readily available in this country. The vet says he can get some, but it will cost £1,500 a month.'

'Wow. I was thinking it would be, maybe, £15 a month. £1,500 is crazy!' said Stewart, clearly wondering what else he could sell. 'How long will she need that?'

'For the rest of her life.'

I don't understand money. I don't see the point of it. People just give me food and toys and all the other stuff I might need, and so I've never had to worry about it. I didn't know if £1,500 a month was a lot or not, but I knew Mary wouldn't want to be let down over a concept that she and I could never understand. Somehow the money would have to be found, and I was determined to help in any way I could. Stewart could even sell all my toys if necessary. But not the squeaky zebra, obviously. We didn't know how long Mary was going to live, but having come so close to dying over the New Year, we all realised that every minute we had with her was a bonus to be cherished and appreciated.

Mary

Yo! It's still Mary here! And that's pretty amazing when you think about it. And you, dearest reader, are amazing too. It's been a privilege and an honour to share my story with you.

I know Pooch has some important things to say, so I'm going to wrap things up by saying that I always loved life. I think I was born with an appreciation of how special it is to be here, and after my illness I love it even more. I may have slowed down a little, and I may not have much time left, but I still love my food and my treats, my toys and my walkies, and I've never lost my gratitude for the most basic things in life, such as having a roof over my head and a family to love me. It really can't get much better than that. Being ill was hard for a while, but the chemo sessions were actually rather good fun. All the veterinary nurses knew me and they loved to cuddle me during my treatments. I actually looked forward to those visits. The drugs made me a little icky for a day or two afterwards, but I would quickly bounce back to full strength. I really am so lucky, and so grateful to my family, the vet, and my puppies for giving me a little more time on this wonderful, joyous planet. Thank you, and you, and you, and

them, and those over there, and them round the
corner, and everyone. Thank you!

Pooch

I'm not a philosopher. I don't even know what philosophers are, although I think I heard somewhere that they're very nice to sit on. Anyway, philosophising not being my thing, I will instead finish on my view of the world and the meaning of life. Oh no, wait. I mean sofas. Very comfy for sitting on. Not philosophers. I'm always mixing those two up. Although Aristotle probably had a nice lap for curling up on... Where was I? Right. The ultimate answer. What it's all about. We are all on this planet together, all sharing the same journey as the earth spins and glides through space. It's like a bus ride that we will never complete. We're born on this bus and we will all die on it. We'll be remembered for a while, and then when the next generation of puppies hop on board to replace us we'll quickly be forgotten.

And the thing is, some dogs on this bus are born, by chance, into the comfy seats where there's room to stretch, there's a buffet and a drinks dispenser, and they're surrounded by dogs and people who embrace them and love them. Others, through no fault of their own, are born into the unheated luggage hold, destined to stay isolated and hungry. Destined to remain in the dark.

So what I say is this: given that we're all sharing this eternal bus trip, perhaps it makes sense to get together and help each other to make the journey a more pleasant experience for everyone. Shuffle a little closer together on our seats to make room for others to join us. Protect the weaklings from the bullies in the back row. Lift up the little ones so they can see the view passing by. Share the food and drink (but keep some of those nice star-shaped biccies for me, please). I haven't researched this thoroughly with numbers and stuff, because with my dubious counting ability I wouldn't get very far, but I think that if everyone slid across their bus seat and made room for one little dog next to them, there would be no more hungry, lonely and homeless dogs in the world, no need for dog shelters, no need for suffering – no need for dogs like Mary to experience the kind of things she went through before I decided to rescue her.

I know, we're not really sharing a bus. You wouldn't catch a pedigree like me riding in one of those things, anyway. I would take a taxi. Or a limousine. What I mean is, we're all on this journey through life together. We'll only get to see the sun above our heads for a short while. Let's all make an effort to ensure that every dog not only gets to see the sun, but to play beneath it, to feel safe and comfortable beneath it, so that when their sun finally sets, they will have a smile on their furry faces.

So, although I am the most important dog in the world, I think it's probably true that every other dog is also the most important. And that's an important thing to remember. Or is it...? I've forgotten what I was talking about.

Epilogue

Pooch

Live fast, forget the second half of the motto – that's my motto. And I have lived fast, and time hasn't hung around for me. It took ages to write this book because Mary, Brando and I were always waiting for Stewart to help with the words, and he's as slow at writing as Brando is at thinking. We've waited so long, in fact, that by the time you read this I'm no longer here. That's right, your darling Pooch who you've obviously by now fallen in love with, has recently and very peacefully passed on. But it's OK. Honestly. I was almost eighteen years old, and in doggy years that's, erm, according to my mathematics, definitely more than one. I was around for a really long time for a dog, and by the end my little body was just worn out. My hearing had gone, my vision was dimming, most of my tiny teeth had been extracted, and I became rather more pungent than usual.

I spent my last days warming my thinning coat in front of a lovely log fire in my living room, getting fed and watered without having to move from my bed, and thinking how lucky I'd been to have the life

I'd led. I now saw how privileged I had been from the beginning.

Obviously, life will never be the same again for my pet humans, but I don't want them to mourn forever. That would be unproductive. Ten, maybe fifteen, years crying constantly and wearing black would be adequate. And then I hope they will open their hearts to another dog, only this time not from a puppy breeder like the one where I came from. I think they should pick an unwanted mutt, starving and lonely somewhere in the world, rather than a pedigree bred for profit. As Mary has shown me, there are far too many of these animals waiting for someone to love them. I hope they take one such animal into their hearts and change its life, like they did for Mary and Brando, and keep the chain of compassion moving forward.

Appendix

The last will and testament of Pooch

I, Pitz, better known as Pooch, being of unsound mind, hereby bequeath all of my worldly wotsits and thingies to my sister Mary and my brother Brando. Specifically, I suppose they could have my bed, but as it's too small for them there's no point. They could have my leads and harnesses, but Mary and Brando are much bigger than me so that wouldn't work either. And they could have my toys, but they've already destroyed them. I haven't saved any of my doggy pocket money, having lost it all in a dodgy investment (a neighbour's cat tricked me into investing in cat food, which he then promptly ate), so what, really, can I leave behind for Mary and Brando? The only thing I can give is the love and attention that Katia and Stewart gave me for all those years. That can now go to my brother and sister. They deserve it. Not as much as I did, but no-one's perfect.

Signed, Pooch xxx

Proudly published by Accent Press

www.accentpress.co.uk